First Blood

These thirteen chilling tales of the supernatural come from the wild and lonely regions of Northumberland, Durham, Westmorland and the Borders – eerie hillsides that for centuries hid lawless fugitives, empty shores that witnessed the savage rites of Celt, Druid and Viking.

Mists from that brutal past, shrieks of the dying, echoes of 'old unhappy far-off things', seep through into the bright present to mystify the characters in F. R. Welsh's hair-raising stories, to terrorize them – even to kill them. The ghosts of blackened criminals swinging on their gibbets; a human sacrifice suspended in an oak tree; the spirits of evil set free from a cathedral tomb at midnight; the inexplicable and bloody death of innocents on Lindisfarne . . . the spine-tingling images which the author conjures up are made more frightening by contrast with the matter-of-fact and sceptical modern world in which he sets them.

Some of these stories are very much in the tradition of M. R. James; others are perhaps in a sharper mould; but all are tales to make the flesh creep, by a new master of the art.

F. R. Welsh

First Blood

Tales of horror
from the Border country

With many thanks
(To a kind hostess

Frank R-W.

June 2015

Constable . London

First published in Great Britain 1985
by Constable and Company Limited
10 Orange Street London WC2H 7EG
Copyright © 1985 by F. R. Welsh
Set in Linotron Plantin 11pt by
Rowland Phototypesetting Limited
Bury St Edmunds, Suffolk
Printed in Great Britain by
St Edmundsbury Press
Bury St Edmunds, Suffolk

British Library CIP data
Welsh, Frank
First blood: tales of horror
from the border country.
I. Title
823'.914[F]   PR6073.E4/

ISBN 0 09 466580 X

Contents

Introduction

These stories of ghosts and the supernatural have one thing in common: they are set in the North of England and the Scottish Borders. The references are to real places, although the names are sometimes disguised, and relate to historical – well, usually historical – events. The Border country has an atmosphere all its own: its inhabitants, who live in the shadow of great relics of the past, are conscious of their traditions with a liveliness rare in other parts of Britain. I was brought up there, at a time when World War II was brewing, and was kept in order by the promise that if I wasn't good the Scots would get me.

The same authenticity cannot be claimed for the entirely spurious scholarship which decorates some stories, nor for the portrayals of individuals. These are altogether fictitious, and when mention is made of any office no resemblance to any holder of it, living, dead or in any other condition, is intended.

Some of my friends and relations, it is true, may recognize in the characters shadowy resemblances to themselves. Where this is so I have spared them a sticky end, especially since they have often been of great help in correcting my more egregious errors.

What is natural and what supernatural? Are not the mountains of the mind as sheer and terrifying as any physical precipice? Are not we all the instruments of our own destruction? Some of these stories have a sting in their tail; some are savage and bloody. The latter accord with the unpleasant times in which we live – times which indicate that the human race is quite as horrible as any invented monster.

My particular thanks are due to Andrew Best for his untiring

7

efforts, and to Agnes Welsh not only for maintaining good relations with the word processor but for most of the agricultural expertise: and to Jon Manchip White for his consistent encouragement.

F.R.W.

1985

First blood

A fine summer day does not guarantee happiness: men and women fret, suffer and die in the sunshine as in the rain, but it cannot be denied that an idyll is much improved by the weather. The summer of 1949 was a good one for idylls. Neil's and Lucy's had started at the sixth form Christmas party. It had been their first term in the sixth and, like their friends, they had spent it in finding their feet and adjusting to the new freedoms. The party had been enlivened by the wicked Alan Redwood, whose father kept the Station Hotel and who had thereby access to the hard stuff, access that was used to sophisticate the soft drinks with an addition of gin. The wicked Alan and his associates had succumbed to their own drink, but Neil and Lucy, both rather proper children, drank only enough to relax their defences and to allow their bodies their own responses. This had happened to an extent that astonished and exhilarated them both.

By the next day they were romantically and hopelessly in love. They were both doing English Literature in the Oxford Higher School Certificate and now, suddenly, they realized what John Donne had been going on about. Christmas, which entailed an unavoidable separation, passed in a happy stupor of the sort that aroused critical comments from the families. The New Year saw them reunited, settling down to doing things together – theatres, concerts, reading the same books from the Literary and Philosophical Society's library – all the delights denied to their unhappy contemporaries in public schools, together with, of course, sex.

By January Neil had Lucy's silver prefect's badge undone

and her white Viyella blouse off: the other garments rapidly followed. With the spring they were able to move to the woods and fields: it was a golden spring. They benefited, although this was before the days of permissiveness and the pill, from an extensive literary acquaintance with sex. The Olympia edition of *Lady Chatterley's Lover* had gone the rounds, they had seen all of Hedy Lamarr in *Extase* at the film club, and they had read the livelier bits of seventeenth-century poetry with priapic pleasure.

Lucy was a happy sensuous girl, and Neil had an amorous inventive streak which served them well enough in place of more advanced instruction. Being children of their times, however, they always stopped short of the final act. This was an object of much serious concern and discussion: there were the examinations to consider – would it perhaps take too much out of them? – and the opinion of their friends – would they be shocked, or was it really required of one? – and of course the possible consequences. Everyone knew what had happened to Thora Lofthouse, who had performed for half the third form, and had a baby in the fourth, and now helped in the British Restaurant in Swalwell, still obliging at weekends.

They finally reached a decision in June, before the mock Higher, lying on Lucy's bed. Neil was nibbling the little golden hairs: he knew that there were other bits he ought to be attending to, but Lucy seemed quite happy with things as they were, so he contented himself with an exploratory lick. This had its effect. Lucy stretched out and caressed his head.

'Does it taste nice?'

'Why don't you try?' He raised his head, moved up, and kissed her. At first a little shocked, Lucy found that it did taste nice. She snuggled closer.

'Do you really love me?'

'Of course I do, you know I do.'

'Then shall we really – you know – *really*? Not now, but very soon – after the mocks. We could go away somewhere together. It wouldn't seem quite right here.'

There was no difficulty in arranging the expedition. The young people had often been away together, although more usually in groups. They either camped or stayed in youth hostels, which had conveyed an air of respectability to parents, and with some reason. There were, after all, separate dormitories, and lubricity among the collective odours of frying bacon and hiking-socks seemed unlikely enough. But Neil and Lucy intended to stay at an hotel, which was something of a different proposition: they had no intention of telling this to their parents.

The question of where to stay had to be considered. This was to be a serious, almost sacramental, occasion, and a trippery tourist resort such as Whitley Bay would be odious. Makers of romantic films wherein sexual congress is represented by waves breaking on a beach had established in their generation an unquestioned link between the two, and they felt proximity to the sea was essential.

The North-east coast is well equipped with small secluded seaside villages from Robin Hood's Bay up to Eyemouth. Many, like Bamburgh, have good small hotels, but for their purposes one was pre-eminently suitable. Holy Island, Lindisfarne, seat of St Cuthbert, cradle of Christianity in England, outpost of civilization, had the true atmosphere of magic, a position in both time and space that was somehow equivocal, poised between the present and all the pasts, as it lay between land and sea, sharing the nature of both, off the long sands of Northumbria.

Its position, only accessible at low tide, and its ruined priory made it ideal. Both of them had visited it, as they had Bamburgh, Dunstanburgh, Warkworth, and the other great sites, but they had never stayed there.

The mock Highers came and went satisfactorily, and the relaxation of discipline that accompanies ends of terms made it easier for them to slip away and include Monday in their weekend. As the time when the great experience was to take place came nearer, Neil grew more tense: would he soon actually be doing it? Would he know what to do? Would everything be all right? Lucy, however, was entirely happy: always a sunny girl, with a friendly disposition, she was glowing with contentment.

It fell to Neil to make all the arrangements. He was leaving nothing to chance on this most important of weekends and had telephoned some days previously to reserve a room at the Manor House Hotel, the only one on the island. He knew that they would normally have expected written notice, but could hardly run the risk of having a confirmation sent to his home. He had at the same time checked the tide-tables for that Saturday, a very necessary precaution when planning a visit to the island, since the causeway was only clear for a couple of hours or so on either side of the low tide. Provided they made an early start, and if the bus was not too late, they would be on time.

When the day came the journey proved a constant irritant to Neil, but Lucy was quite unperturbed, letting nothing worry her. She had in her own mind cast the dice and was now content to wait upon events. Neil had to hurry her from the Marl-borough Street bus station, where they left the bus from Ryton, to the Haymarket which served the long-distance buses to Scotland. Lucy showed a disposition to look in shop windows, although in that year of continuing austerity there was little to see, and had trouble with her sandals.

But they were on time and the bus was on time – Neil had a schedule which he checked at the successive stops as it made its way through pit villages to the rich Northumberland farmland, past the story-book castle of Alnwick, economically guarded by its stone men-at-arms, to their destination, the Plough Inn on the Great North Road, not far short of Berwick, where taxis waited to take visitors to the island. Taxis that were unlike any others, with raised and strengthened suspension to help them over the shallows, bodies pitted and corroded by years of salt spray, and very little in the way of interior fittings. It was necessary to make the mile-long country-lane journey from main road to the causeway very gently, but then the taxis came into their own and bucketed steadily through the deepening pools formed by the rising tide. The causeway, such as it was, had marker poles, and near the middle was a refuge, held above high-tide level on stilts, where travellers caught by the sea could spend a safe, if unpleasant, few hours.

After the causeway was negotiated, the taxi crossed another section of sand before the buildings of the island came in sight, seeming to move between the dunes, the small stone houses terminating at one end in the great ruins of the priory, and at the other in the smooth bulk of the castle raised like a warship or a stranded whale from the low line of sand. The hotel, a substantial grey stone building which was the largest house on the island and had in fact been the manor house, faced Neil with his greatest problem, that of negotiating the receptionist. This turned out to be an unnecessary apprehension: a cheery motherly body to whom other peoples' business was a matter of little concern gave him a key and popped back to the kitchen from whence she had come.

Their room was everything it should be; a sea view south to the Farnes, a picture of Grace Darling, and best of all a large and capacious double bed. Neil felt that he had done well, but they were by now too cramped after their journey and too hungry to take advantage of it. Besides, both came from a culture where beds were used only at night, and the idea of daytime love-making even on a bed seemed somehow improper and decadent.

It was much too late to lunch at the hotel, and the only other place where food might be had was the pub next to the Priory; indeed, it should have been too late even for that, had licensing hours been observed, but the islanders, at least when the tide was in, were not much concerned with such details. Since there was no policeman on the island, what the landlords and drinkers did at those times was the subject of mutual agreement, and the agreement at weekends was to stay open.

One of the bars was crowded with young men and a few girls, grubby and noisy, their thick Glasgow accents incomprehensible to any outsider. The landlord had given up any attempt to clear the bar and empty bottles filled every table. His expression suggested he was nearing the end of his patience with the Glaswegians, but he served Neil and Lucy willingly with hot pies, brown ale and a cider for Lucy. Neil did not really like beer, but he was going through a phase of reading Belloc and felt that he should, so persevered although he knew quite well he would much rather have drunk cider too.

For the rest of the day they explored the island. They puzzled out the remains of the priory with the help of the Ministry of Works plan, examined St Cuthbert's hermitage, and walked along the beach to the castle. Although looking magnificently medieval, this had in fact been built in the sixteenth century by Henry VIII as a stone man-of-war to discourage French or Scots from approaching the coast, at a time when the Auld Alliance might have been invoked by the Scots reeling under the defeats of Flodden and Halidon Hill. Neil and Lucy were not only doing Modern History from 1489 for Higher, but, being Borderers, had their own special knowledge of Border conflict, and could have given the dates of every fight from Solway Moss onwards.

The beach was no spot for bathing or making sand-castles but the workplace of the island community. On the marram grass above the high-water mark the fishermen had made shelters for their tackle by overturning old boat-hulls and patching them with driftwood and tar. Fish-boxes and rusty windlasses lay scattered about, while further down the beach were the boats themselves, gaily painted blue, green, white, yellow and red, the cobles of the North-east coast. These interesting vessels are peculiar to that region, from Berwick to Whitby, and are unlike any boat found elsewhere. They are built with broad strakes giving an odd geometric section, with sharp tumblehome and broad beam. Their fine sterns are cut off with a transom and their deep forefoot gives a high bow. Although entirely open they will cope with the worst, or very nearly the worst, that the North Sea can hand out, which can be very bad indeed. When

Henry Greathead invented the lifeboat at South Shields, it was the sea-keeping qualities of the coble that he copied. Until diesels came into common use, they were rowed or sailed with a dipping lug; enthusiasts still sometimes use them as sailing-boats, and very effective, although uncomfortable, they are.

It is said that cobles are, like the Shetland sixerns, descendants of the Viking longboats adapted for working off the Northumbrian beaches rather than more northerly fjords; it is certainly difficult to imagine a tougher or safer open boat ever being devised.

Further up the beach, back on a level with the huts, was a curiosity. A brand new coble had been built, and, her paintwork shining, was poised on chocks ready to be slid into the water at the next springs. She was one of the biggest, nearly forty feet long, with her high stern rising eight feet from the ground, all white inboard, with a green and blue hull.

Dinner at seven was predictably but excellently fishy, and left the two young people replete and affectionate, although it was much too early to go to bed with any semblance of decency. Since they did not want to become involved in chatting to fellow guests, in case reports of their presence there might be passed back home, or to listen to the Home Service on the wireless, and since only a crescent moon gave any light at all, making moonlight rambles difficult, there was little for it but another visit to the pub.

As they walked, amiably hand in hand, they knew all the calm certainty of lovers. The clouds fleetingly obscured the moon but not the occulting flashes from the Outer Farnes light, and to the north the loom of the Berwick light could be seen. There was enough light streaming through the clouds to see the gaunt outlines of the priory ruins contrasting with the cheerful aspect of the village.

As soon as they opened the door the happy indolent and expectant mood of the day was shattered. They made for the bar they had used earlier, but as they went inside they saw it to be packed with the Glaswegians, who had clearly been drinking all day. The room was full of dirty glasses, foul with cigarette-smoke and noisy with raucous and aggressive voices: one or two bodies were slumped across tables, dead drunk.

Neil shut the door and went into the other bar, which had been tidied and was now almost empty. The landlord was looking unhappy. 'Aa divvin' min telling you a'm pleased its low tide at closing time and A'll be shot of this lot before they're any dafter.'

Neil could not help thinking there was quite enough time left for them to become a great deal dafter, when one lurched into the bar and staggered over to him. He was older, but not a great deal older, than Neil, smaller, dirty in an entrenched fashion, in an army battledress blouse, navy trousers and filthy canvas shoes. His hair was thick with cream and his ears full of brown wax. 'So, we're not guid enough for you and yon wee hairie,' he shouted. When Neil, embarrassed rather than frightened, did not answer, the youth grabbed him by his jacket and shouted with an effluxion of disgusting breath: 'I'll show ye who's guid enough.'

The hand on Neil's lapel was small, warty, the fingernails bitten to extinction. It was also unpleasantly wet, giving the impression of having been in unpleasant places handling un-pleasant things. Neil was still embarrassed rather than apprehensive, but felt the hand was too nasty to be tolerated. His only experience of violence had been in school scraps, years ago, and he had no clear idea of what was expected of him. Argument would not serve, and he could not bear the idea of having to grasp that filthy hand if he was to remove it. A memory of playground tactics came to him. 'Please take your hand away,' – there had always to be a proffered olive branch.

The olive branch was rejected, as was expected, and the riposte 'Fo'in piece o' snot . . .' was cut short by a quick knee in the groin from Neil.

It worked quite alarmingly well; the youth collapsed on the

floor, writhing and spewing, but managing some loud obsceni-
ties between gasps. The adjoining door opened and some of the
others looked in. Seeing their comrade sprawling on the floor
they started for Neil, shouting for revenge: one had a beer
bottle grasped by the neck. Neil was now, and rightly, very
frightened: he looked around for a way of escape. Lucy,
horrified had already backed towards the outside door when it
opened.

The man who came in was the most impressive and most
welcome person Neil had ever seen. He was massively solid, his
face red-brown, seamed and wrinkled like an elephant or
rhinoceros, and appearing no less armoured. He must have
weighed twenty stone, very little of it superfluous. He wore
dungarees, a fisherman's gansey, and a tweed cap; his feet were
clad in carpet slippers. Looking neither at Neil nor his victim,
now painfully rising, nor at his menacing friends, he walked
straight over to the bar and asked for ginger beer. The youths,
who had fallen momentarily silent, began to shout abuse in
their weird accents at this token of softness.

The large man looked at the landlord, who nodded. He
turned deliberately towards the Scotsmen. 'You'll be better off
next door, laddies.'

They took no notice, and the one with the beer bottle moved
towards Neil. 'Had yer gob aud man, he hut wee Jamie, he did.
And a'll smash his face in.' The big man, moving like a panther
for all his size, stepped quickly between them. He took the
hand holding the broken bottle, quite gently, and squeezed.
The young Scot's face went white, he shrank back, the bottle
fell.

'That's enough for the neet, now, be off all of you: and don't
have any ideas about hanging about outside.' It was enough: the
lads slunk off, subdued and sobered. The man was something
outside their experience, but they understood he was not to be
tampered with.

'And if I were you, young man, I'd wait here a little,' he said
turning to Neil, 'and let them take themselves right off.'

17

The landlord grinned for the first time. 'It is a right relief knowing Thomas is next door when there's a bit o' bother likely: I got the word sent when that young rapscallion showed his face.'

'Aye,' sighed Thomas, 'I don't hold with violence, nor drunkenness.' He looked old-fashionedly at the landlord. 'There's enough wickedness in the world as it is, and enough fear and death to be found a hundred yards out t'sea, without adding to't gratuitously.' He spoke with a broad Northumbrian burr, trilling his r's in the way his countrymen have done since the days of Harry Hotspur, and enjoying the fine word, another North-eastern characteristic.

Thomas settled in front of the fire, making way for the two young people to sit alongside in the privileged position: even in July the island nights were cool enough to make a driftwood blaze welcome. Neil, compromising between Belloc and Thomas, ordered a shandy; he felt that another literary drinking problem had been solved, and wondered what he should do about Zola and absinthe.

Lucy, who had been shaken by the episode, was reassured by the bulk of Thomas and the comforting incongruity between his massive strength and the ginger beer and carpet slippers. She tried the shandy and immediately liked it, tucked her feet up, and prepared to listen to Thomas, who showed himself appreciative of the audience. He told them of his life out fishing, when the weather allowed, with lines for cod and mackerel, nets for the bottom fish, pots for the lobsters that brought such high prices when the luck was in, and the occasional turbot sent straight to the hotels in London: it was a hard life in the winter, and lonely too, so summer visitors provided a bit of variety. Lucy was fascinated by his description of the birds that followed the boat, the seals with their pups, and the porpoises playing. Neil contemplated a Hardyesque novel of Northumbrian life, with a younger Thomas disappointed in love as its central character.

When all was quiet outside Thomas walked them both back

to the hotel, just in case. He paused for a moment before saying, 'Why, ah've got tae see tae the pots in the morning. Mebbe ye'd like a wee trip in the coble? We'd be sure to see some birds, and likely the seals will be aboot?'

Lucy and Neil were very happy to accept what seemed a timely and serendipitous invitation, and made off to bed. The fresh air and the excitements of the day had, however, been too much for them, and, rather to their surprise in the morning, both fell almost instantly asleep, hand in hand in their big bed.

Breakfast in the Manor House was a serious and sustaining meal; they did full justice to Weetabix, bacon, sausage and egg, toast and tea – they were too wise in the ways of the world to believe that drinkable coffee could be found outside Newcastle. After breakfast they walked through the churchyard before meeting Thomas on the beach. It was still early enough for sea fret to obscure the details, and the ruins of the abbey were spectral in the luminous mist.

Thomas's boat was one of the smaller cobles, but with a good diesel engine, riding the waves like a seabird. Once they were outside the difficult entrance to the bay, Neil was given the helm while Thomas, who was proving a great talker, talked.

He displayed a wide knowledge of the history of the coast, and a great affection for its inhabitants, identifying for Lucy's benefit the huddles of guillemots that scattered as their boat approached, startled puffins with their parrot-like beaks skimming the waves, dozing eider ducks that looked at them and sedately swam away, cormorants which, running along the water, took off in an untidy fashion. But most of all Lucy loved the terns and gannets as they dived into the water with grace and elegance.

To their starboard the bulk of Bamburgh Castle solidified out of the mist. 'Lancelot's castle of Joyous Gard, they say that was,' remarked Thomas, 'and one of King Arthur's battles was fought near here. Mind you, that's as much legend as history, if not a bit more so. They couldn't keep the Saxons off for long, and after them the Vikings came from Scandinavia. Bloody folk

19

they were!' Thomas dealt with the Vikings at some length, they being a favourite subject of his. 'They were people of the sea first and last – Viking means "man of the bays" – and their ships were the finest ever made. They sacked the coasts of France and Spain, and sailed down the Russian rivers right to Constantinople, dragging the ships behind them. A bit later, after they'd settled down in Northern France for a hundred years or so, they became more civilized, and set up their kingdoms from Scotland to Palestine. But in the early days they were a wild lot.

'It was in the summer of 793 that they came to the island and plundered the church, killing everything they could lay their hands on. It really shook England, that did, for Lindisfarne was one of the holiest places and they desecrated it thoroughly. Very nasty habits they had, and a lot of them, especially the ones with the horses, I wouldn't want to tell a young lady about.

'But they knew all about ships and the sea, the Vikings. Lovely things their boats were – you can see one of them still, over at Oslo. These cobles are the nearest things to them otherwise: look at the high prow on this little one – you can imagine it with a dragon head. The stern's been altered for the beaches, but they're still real Viking ships.

'On the Day of Judgement – only they didn't call it that, being heathen, but Ragnarok – they thought that a great ship would come, packed with giants and monsters from Hel – that was one of the Viking ideas, Hell, only they spelled it differently. She was called Naglfar, that ship, and was made all out of dead mens' nails. The ships were right at the centre of all their legends and superstitions.

'And a lot of those got taken over by the Christians: holy places aren't holy only to one religion. The new priests took over the old holy wells and groves and called them after saints. It might be that people were just used to them or it might be that there was really something strange and powerful about the places themselves. It was the same with ships, which were sacred to them. When we break a bottle of champagne over the bows of a ship at the launch, that's a libation, a sacrifice to the gods that's gone on ever since those days. Only they sacrificed more than wine. Animals mostly, but the pagan Vikings used to run the new ships down to the water over the bodies of slaves.'

Lucy gave a shudder at this, then laughed. 'But they have to be content with champagne now that they're Christians.'

That restored the spirits of the young ones, who had become a little subdued at the misdeeds of the Vikings. As soon as they landed on the Longstone, everything was forgotten except the seals and the birds. Thomas had given them a bird identification book, and got lunch ready while the two explored. It was quite late when they returned, more like tea-time really, and Lucy was very excited at having spotted twenty-three different species, to say nothing of the seals.

That night, after saying good-bye to Thomas and promising to pay another visit in the autumn, they avoided the pub and went for a long walk, ending up on the fishing beach beside the boats and huts. It was a warmer night, although the breeze was present, and forsaking the prospect of the double bed they lay down in the shelter of the new coble.

Their love-making was brisk and urgent; it was not long before Lucy was stretched out, legs apart and thighs raised, in an attitude she found new, abandoned, but completely right. As Neil raised himself gently above her she gasped in luxurious anticipation and stretched out her arms, striking one of the props that held the coble.

The solicitor and police surgeon were walking along the north pier at Berwick, watching the sleek heads of the seals that had come in with the tide. There was something they did not want to talk about, but they felt a compulsion, as if to scratch at a sore.

'Nasty business on the Island, Tim.' The solicitor felt he must make a beginning.

'As nasty as anything I have seen, and it might even be a little nastier. You've no proof as to what happened?'

'Not a shadow. The police thought it might have been those tearaways from over the Border, and gave them a very hard time of it, but couldn't find any proof. They put that old Tom Clegg through it, too: he'd spent all day with the children, and he's a bit queer, but he was in the pub at the time and seemed very shaken by the news. It's true there was a breeze, but not that strong. They might have knocked a prop away, but everyone swears that a twenty-ton boat wouldn't move because of that. You couldn't find anything to go on the medical evidence?'

'Nothing I cared to put forward, but, something really rather odd. The boat had crushed the upper parts of the bodies very badly, pretty much inextricably, in fact, but the legs and pelvis were more or less undamaged, except for lacerations where they had been dragged over the beach as the boat rolled on into the sea. I'm not disturbing you, am I?'

'I can't say I relish the detail, but go on.'

'Well, I was able to establish that the girl was *virgo intacta*: I don't think that she would have been so in a few minutes' time, from all indications, but she died a maid nevertheless. I didn't say anything, since it seemed pointless, but you know those old stories about ships, and how the Vikings launched them? They said they always preferred virgins. Well, this boat got one, but only just.'

The red kite

There are places in England, reflected Stillinfleet, contemplating his beer, where the bones of the country lie very near the surface. Ancient evidences – standing stones, earthworks, Roman roads, old battlefields – are still prominent features, not overlaid by the newer landscape of agriculture, drainage, or the removal of forests. History is a living tradition among such men as the old miners in the public bars, whose forebears have lived in the same village for generations. (The same might be thought true of Ireland, but in that inward-looking, self-regarding country, the ancient facts have been overlaid by misty fiction and self-dramatization; what can be seen are not the clear, if damaged, proofs of history, but objects prayed as aid in evidence of contradictory myths.)

As it is, this phenomenon is to be found in its most marked form in the north of England. Physical remains abound – Hadrian's Wall, the palace of Yeavering Bell, Ewe Close and its neighbouring Celtic village, their doorsteps and lintels still in place, and the churches where Bede, Wilfred and Alcuin worshipped. The people are still quiet Saxons and Danes with a touch of Viking wildness but with an un-Celtic pragmatism which enables them to live contentedly with their past.

The Dun Cow in the city of Durham was an apt place to prompt such thought. It was Stillinfleet's custom to pay it a visit about opening time each morning, a custom that had begun when, as a junior lecturer, he had been given the unpopular nine and ten o'clock stints – a good medieval word, still part of the working vocabulary of northern miners and shepherds – and had, after two hours of instruction of the young, stood

23

much in need of refreshment. Now, as Reader in Medieval Studies at the University of Durham, he had few such tedious duties, but continued his regular potations, and had become accustomed to the permanently raised eyebrows of some of his colleagues at what might be accounted unconventional behaviour. The frequenting of taverns by clerks had been a custom of universities since the thirteenth century, and he felt entirely justified in continuing it.

Besides, he had a meeting with the Dean in prospect and required fortification against an encounter he did not expect to be propitious.

A second pint thus justified and disposed of, Stillinfleet left the inn, turning down the steps leading to the river. Above him rose the cliffs supporting the enormous bulk of the cathedral, forming one of the great sights of Europe. The drama of the west front rising straight from the cliff face never failed to thrill him. It was the ultimate expression of one aspect of the Norman spirit, a massive assertion of power, marking with a brutal finality the northern-most point of their European invasion – as Palermo, in its more ornate and elegant fashion, marks the southern.

As he began the climb towards the plateau the Galilee Chapel came into view. Durham Cathedral is unique in many ways, and among the most obvious is its lack of a west door: this would anyway be redundant, since the West front gives straight on to the cliff above the river. Where the door would have been there is a Lady Chapel, the Galilee, placed there a century after the cathedral was begun. It is said that it was built as far away from the main altar and the tomb of St Cuthbert as possible, out of deference to the saint's well-known dislike of women, but, be that as it may, the terrible things that took place that night had the Galilee as their centre, and it is important to understand the nature of the place. The contrast with the solid mass of the nave could not be more striking: the Galilee is all airy elegance, much more like Sicily than Northumbria. Pevsner says of the light within that one feels as though one were out of doors; Stillinfleet always thought it subaqueous, rather, but agreed that the whole effect was one of light and space after the dramatic chiaroscuro of the nave's bulk.

The interior of the chapel is free of that clutter of centuries that mar our cathedrals; the dominating object is a sarcophagus sealed with a simple slab of black marble inscribed, '*Hac sunt in fossa Bedae venerabilis ossa*', the tomb for more than a thousand years of the Venerable Bede. Again, since the story of Bede is entirely germane to the events of that night, it will bear repeating.

Bede was one of those good men whose virtues shone effulgently in the Dark Ages in which they lived – free from prejudice, equal-minded, gentle, cultivated, loving, devoid of ambition, and the greatest scholar of the time, he was honoured in his lifetime, and on his death his monastery of Jarrow became a place of pilgrimage. Some centuries later a priest of Durham, one Alfred, became jealous of Jarrow's popularity. Alfred seems to have spent his life stealing relics in order to attract worshippers to his own church, and he carried off Bede's remains to place them in the tomb already occupied by St Cuthbert. When Bishop Pudsey built the Galilee in 1170 he had Bede's body placed there in a magnificent coffin. At the 'Reformation' the casket was stolen, but the body, still wrapped as it had been when the acquisitive Alfred took it from Jarrow, was left.

The tomb is still a popular place, although now perhaps in a less reverential and more affectionate way than in the days of devotion. When the service for the Miners' Gala is held in June, few omit to pay their good-humoured respects to the most famous of Northumbrians.

Bede's death – and again this is a matter of some importance – is one of the best documented of the Dark Ages; the circumstances are recorded, in detail, in a letter from his pupil Cuthbert to a friend, Cuthwin. Cuthbert also recorded Bede's lectures which continued to the day of his death, as well as details of everyday conversations. One of Bede's amiable habits was a fondness for repeating poetry he had learned in his

25

boyhood, a touching and timeless attribute. The poetry was often Anglo-Saxon, and one such poem bade man remember:

> *Before he need go forth,*
> *None can be too wise in thinking*
> *How before his soul can go*
> *What good or ill deeds he hath done,*
> *How after death his doom shall be.*

'How after death his doom shall be' is a line quite peculiarly applicable to this story.

Cuthbert tells us that Bede died about eight in the evening on 26 May 735, an extremely accurate and reliable date (it was Ascension Day), and it was, as it happens, exactly this point which sparked off the whole affair.

Stillinfleet, was, characteristically, a few minutes late in arriving for his appointment, and found the Dean and his guests deep in the matter in hand.

The Dean of Durham's study is, as befits so senior a cleric, an imposing apartment looking out on to the College Green. Dean Robinson had furnished it with considerable care, and with the aid of many consultations with that admirable firm, Messrs Watts of Westminster; a Burges wallpaper was muted by chaste green curtains with a Gothick border; leather shelf-edgings hid any irregularities – irregularities of size only, of course – among the Dean's books; and the furniture, all of the same mid-century period, was both seemly and useful.

His two guests wore the room as though it were their natural habitat, with that ability to blend into a background that is often enjoyed by American academics in the course of their field studies. Professor Arnison was a real, head-of-department professor at a very respectable Virginia-creeper (if not quite Ivy League) university, and Dr Grattan a graduate of both that university and the Cambridge-in-exile, Yale. Both were becomingly seated on upright armchairs upholstered in rather too shiny leather.

Stillinfleet muttered something that could charitably be taken as an apology and sank into a low armchair, his knees higher than his chin, in a discordantly un-Victorian attitude, displaying all that weary scepticism, occasioned by constant exposure to the differences between human pretensions and the sordid facts of human behaviour, that may be observed in historians of the Age of Faith. The purport of the conference was to discuss the Americans' application to be permitted access to the Bede tomb in order to try a newly developed age-dating test. While this would usually be out of the question, their eminence ensured the Americans' case a hearing, and Stillinfleet sensed that Dean Robinson, who was more distinguished for administrative than academic talents, would appreciate seeing his own name on their eventual research paper. He began to enjoy the Dean's unaccustomed indecision.

'Of course, Professor, I recognize the scientific, and indeed the historical, importance of your work, but disturbing a sepulchre, especially one of this eminence, is always, at least . . .' The Professor took advantage of the Dean's momentary, and it should be said, unusual loss of the correct word. He had been in danger of saying 'a grave responsibility' and only avoided the trap at the last moment.

'But Dean, the authenticity or otherwise of the Turin Shroud is, if I might say so with the greatest of possible respect, more than a matter of scientific or historical importance: it touches, does it not, the very basis of the Christian faith? If the Shroud is indeed an artefact of the first century, we may well be in the presence of a miracle. And for the first time we have the techniques available to determine this matter beyond a peradventure.'

'And to do this, you need a reference point?' This was Stillinfleet's first contribution to the discussion: he was by now surfeited with the Dean's discomfort.

Professor Arnison sensed a potential ally and turned his capacity for exegesis on Stillinfleet. 'Say rather, sir, a multiplicity of co-ordinates. It might be said that there is an analogy in time to a navigational exercise in space. The precision with which we can define our unknown is a function of fixed points we can establish.'

'The more samples the better?'

'Provided that they can be dated exactly by historical reference, that will verify our test methods. We are confident that we can predicate age by our tests, but the proof of this is only to be gained over a number of trials.'

'And the Bede cere-cloth is just such a sample?'

The second visitor, Dr Grattan, felt that as another historian he could better understand Stillinfleet, and was therefore justified in interposing. 'Of most outstanding importance, Dr Stillinfleet.' He shared the common misapprehension of American academics that a doctorate was obligatory to aspirants for university office. 'It is well attested that the external wrapping of Bede's body, over the linen shroud, is of Byzantine silk from the Imperial mills, purchased by the monastery two years before Bede's death: it would have been spun no more than five years prior to that date. The shroud itself we may assume to be contemporaneous with Bede's original interment, and we are confident that our testing procedures will enable us to confirm this within an accuracy of twelve months, at the most.'

'The actual date is significant,' interjected the Professor, who had no intention of letting historians intermeddle unduly in what was fundamentally a scientific matter, 'since we have a number of silk samples from the tenth century onwards, and extrapolation from these dates back to the eighth century will give us a scale of differentiation.'

'And then,' said the Dean, 'you will have enough evidence to convince the Turin authorities to let you make a thorough examination of the Shroud itself?'

The Professor replied with measured authority that such an undertaking had been given, providing the tests on the Bede cere-cloth were confirmatory of their methods. During the conversation Stillinfleet had moved to an almost vertical position, an act so unusual as to signal clearly to the Dean that his interest had been stirred. He rummaged in several pockets before producing pipe, tobacco and matches, at which the Professor, a fervent non-smoker, looked disapproving, a disapprobation that did not perturb its object who was about to make a pronouncement.

'In the ordinary way of things I wouldn't like the idea of messing about with the old boy at all – there's a history you may know of, Dean – but if there's a chance of exposing that Turin Shroud mummery for the nonsense it is – like flying houses of Loreto, blood of St Januarius! Bat-shit!'

The expletive referred, of course, to the received explanation of the latter phenomenon. It was one of Stillinfleet's most favoured terms of abuse for whatever he took to be superstition and credulity, and was as likely to be employed against monetarists or Marxists as against the devout.

'You need have no apprehension as to the safety of the operation,' said the Professor reassuringly, and, as it transpired, mistakenly, 'for our methods necessitate the removal of only quite microscopic fragments, only a few milligrams. As you doubtless know, the carbon-dating methods all depend on isolating the isotope carbon-14 and diverting the radiation emitted therefrom. We, by contrast, separate the carbon-14 from the much more common carbon-12 isotope, and the resultant mix, which we quantify by spectromical methodology, enables us to accurately, and with the minimum of disturbance to the original artefact, date the sample with the finest of precision.'

So monstrously split an infinitive left the Dean momentarily speechless, and hastened the conclusion of the discussion.

With Stillinfleet sympathetic, or at least not obstreperously antipathetic, the experiment was agreed upon. In the interests of secrecy the sample would be taken at night, with only the Professor and Dr Grattan there, and Stillinfleet going along 'to see fair play by the Venerable,' a point on which he insisted. Since there was no point in procrastination, the work was to be done that night. Even the mention of the bats, although indelicate, was useful, since it was decided that the ostensible purpose of the expedition, which had to be given to the cathedral security office, would be nocturnal photography of the building's bats.

The Americans, although invited, chose not to dine at the Deanery. They were naturally excited by the prospect of gaining their sample and were anxious to spend what time they had checking their equipment and 'probably devouring some Big Colonel Pizza from a take-home,' according to Stillinfleet, whose views of American eating-habits were both confused and hostile; although in fact the visitors were to eat a quite proper, if expensive, dinner in the Royal County Hotel.

Their equipment was complex enough to merit attention, especially since it was only for the purpose of taking the sample; the real testing was, of course, to be carried out in their own laboratory. What they had with them was capable of being packed into a small suitcase, and included an aluminium folding scaffold, something like a small Scotch derrick with a winch, to take the weight of the giant slab, graphite grease to allow it to be removed more easily, tripod-mounted and hand-held torches, tools to remove the lead and wood of the coffin, should that be necessary, surgical instruments to separate and handle the fabric, which must not be touched, together with a carrying-case for the fabric, and even a miniature vacuum-cleaner to remove any trace of their activities.

The Dean and Stillinfleet dined alone; and with that comfortable glow that comes with the savoury at collegiate dinners the Dean raised a question. 'You may recall mentioning a history, something of a similar nature?'

The question caused Stillinfleet some embarrassment. He was by now much looking forward to the prospect of a little modest sacrilege, all in the cause of rationalism, and the story he had mentioned was, well, uncomfortable.

'Oh, it was in the early years of last century, someone tried something similar, I believe, although of course quite illegally, and it didn't turn out too well. Are these angels or devils, these things?'

'Angels, my dear Stillinfleet: they contain oysters, and are the superior comestible. Devils have prunes within the bacon, and are not, to my mind, a fitting article of nourishment. But your story?'

'Well, it was all fairly firmly hushed up at the time. It concerned a local amateur ecclesiologist, one Forster or Forrester, who was a respectable grain merchant and factor by trade. He took it into his head to do a little private research. At least, they found the sarcophagus lid displaced in the morning and assumed he had secreted himself in the chapel when it closed the evening before. He made a poor job of it – you can still see two small chips on the under edge where he put his crowbars.'

The Dean sensed a reluctance and was implacable. 'And what exactly transpired?'

'From what was pieced together afterwards – the man himself was in no condition to be of any assistance – it seemed that he had been caught up in the Tractarian movement. He had a chapel in his house, was keen on reviving all sorts of rituals, and had the right kit for everything. Rather like the monk Alfred, wild about relics, and had collected quite a number himself, but rather second-division stuff – bits of stone from Walsingham, handkerchiefs from some bishop or another; probably wanted something a little more worthy of muttering over. Anyway, there in the morning was the tomb opened – only a foot or so – and Forster! Well, he was discovered, rather dramatically, clutching the sanctuary knocker on the north door. They had a job prising him away from it, and he never uttered a sensible word from that day on. Of course, he was pretty well gone before it started – religious mania exacerbated by passing a night alone in the cathedral. Of course, equally, things being as they were in the Church at that time, everybody was anxious to ensure that nothing got out.'

'It would have been one in the eye for the Oxford men, certainly.' The Dean was an Arminian of decidedly Whiggish tendencies. 'I can, I am sure, trust that neither you, my dear, nor those American friends of yours, will be in danger of any religious excesses destabilizing, as they themselves would doubtless put it, your own equilibrium.'

Be that as it may, when Stillinfleet let himself into the cathedral by the north door that evening, he found his hand reaching out to stroke the worn bronze of the sanctuary knocker. For eight hundred years it had been an object of power: any man, of whatever crimes he might stand accused, who managed to evade his pursuers and reach the cathedral, even by touching symbolically the knocker of the door, was safe. The Church had him in her protection, and if he undertook the appropriate penances and performed the appointed rites, a safe exile was assured to him. What pursuers had Forster been fleeing, Stillinfleet wondered, and was not surprised to feel himself shiver. It was a cold night, and here he was loitering about!

He entered the cathedral, and was absorbed into the enormous dark space of the nave. He paused, and was conscious of the hundred tiny noises of the night; stone and wood cooling and settling, a draught stirring the dusty regimental banners, small insects, birds, and even the useful bats, going about their diverse businesses.

After the majestic emptiness of the nave the Galilee seemed intimate and almost domestic. The scientists were already there, absorbed in their tasks, and gave him only a scant and cursory welcome. They had rigged their nautical-looking block-and-tackle; nylon cords attached to rubber bands spanning the lid of the sarcophagus led through a single ring to the tackle, and thence to the winch which was secured in turn to a pillar. A steady pull on this would raise the lid and keep it checked on the ratchet.

Arnison stood at the head of the tomb with a number of plastic cylinders and a slender crowbar of stainless steel. As Grattan took the pressure on the winch, the sharp end of the bar was slid into the crack between the slab and the sides of the tomb, and as this widened the joint was raked out and the cylinders slid into place. On these rollers, inch by inch, the lid moved forward until two feet of the interior of the sarcophagus was exposed. Grattan then checked the winch and moved to the side of Arnison, who was peering into the tomb with a pencil-torch while operating the small vacuum-cleaner. Grattan was holding a notebook and the sample box: Stillinfleet had settled himself into a convenient niche and was watching the scene, which was patchily illuminated by the flashlights and the two flexible spotlights placed on the slab.

He was feeling a little smug at the time, since he had provided himself with the one piece of modern technology that the Americans seemed to have forgotten – a tape recorder: this he switched on, and much of what we know of the subsequent events is due to the fact that the pocket instrument was kept running during all that occurred and beyond, until its batteries ran out.

The first voice that can be heard on the tape is Arnison's, as he bent over the sepulchre. 'Oh my, a great deal of dust . . . spiders seem to have been busy . . . that's better . . . lead quite perished, just to be expected . . . pieces of wood . . . why, I do believe here's a fragment of cloth all ready for us . . . yes . . . are you ready [the tape is a little muffled here as Arnison and Grattan transferred their find to the sample case] . . . just a mite further . . . we'd best make sure it's the real thing . . . That's strange . . . bring a light would you . . . yes . . . isn't that more lead? Do you think there could have been a second burial? I'll just try with the crowbar . . .'

There follows a pause, and after that no more words are recorded, only noises – and what noises! I have heard the tape once myself, and nothing would make me ever play it again, yet I cannot believe that it should be destroyed: if there is anything worse than knowing the truth about terrible things it is that invincible ignorance which denies the existence of those hor-rors. Sudden violence, even when expected, comes very quick-ly: the bottle broken on the bar and thrust in the face; the

33

trigger slipping and the shot fired when nothing was foreseen; the friendly cat turning on the instant, to scratch. The eruption of noise on the tape has all these qualities, besides the anguish of the noises themselves.

They are indescribable except by analogy, and an analysis can give only a measure of their beastliness. Taking into account what was found afterwards, it seems that once the fit, or whatever it was, took hold of Arnison, and he started his screaming chant, he must have bludgeoned the miserable Grattan to the ground with the crowbar, striking him helpless, but tragically not senseless, for the other noises, those that I can hear still at the bad times, make it clear that he was only too horribly conscious. Arnison must have then – and we know this from the bloodstains – torn off his own clothes, all his own clothes – and Grattan's coat and shirt, all the while shrieking his fearful rhythmic chant.

It is best to say quite plainly what happened, and leave the imagination to construct the noises, the appalling noises that accompanied them. Arnison threw his victim face down, and, using the crowbar, hacked at his back, breaking and chopping the ribs from the spine, forcing them up through the skin, until he was able to plunge his hands into the chest cavity, and, tearing out the lungs, to spread them on the naked ruined back. And all this time – you can hear the noises – Grattan was alive.

The noises stop, and there is a pause. Arnison, and the thing that had been released from the tomb to master him, were looking around for Stillinfleet.

Of course it couldn't be hushed up entirely but they did very well, all things considered. Arnison, they gave out, had, in a fit of homicidal mania, murdered Grattan – they were able to suppress the nasty bits – and in a fit of remorse had committed suicide by throwing himself off the clerestory walk. He was certainly found there, on the floor of the nave, having smashed half a dozen chairs before coming suddenly to rest. Such an explanation will hardly satisfy you, being in possession of all the facts. My own is not incompatible with the official version, but goes into the question the other begs: what touched off the madness?

We have to go back to the source of the trouble, the tomb. After Bede's death the stable kingdom of Northumbria was subjected to Viking raids: these were stoutly resisted – you remember the uncomfortable end devised by King Aella for Ragnar Leatherbreeks, the Viking leader? – but this resistance only inflamed the ferocity of the raiders. Some of these men were savage almost beyond belief: the Baresarkers, or Berserkers, charged into battle naked, believing themselves invulnerable. One of their favourite methods of killing a captured enemy was by tearing out his lungs and exposing them on his back like the wings of a bird: they called this 'flying the red kite'. It is not inconceivable that one of these Vikings, captured by the Northumbrians – it might have been Ragnar himself – and put to death in the most painful fashion they could devise, might have made himself troublesome after death. If a good and gentle man like Bede can for centuries afterwards engender a feeling of peace and tranquillity, a pitiless and criminal man might do quite the opposite. It might well have appealed to the logical medieval mind to neutralize the mischief by placing the evil remains under those of Bede, and letting the good suppress the evil; until, that is, some over-curious person opened the tomb and let it out. The balance of the human psyche is always precarious and can be upset by a great number of ill-defined influences. The suggestion is fortified, as you will agree, by some aspects of the incident – to which one might add another detail, that Arnison is a Scandinavian name. I do believe that I am the only person living who has heard a tenth-century Berserker war song.

And Stillinfleet? Oh, he survived, rather the worse for wear, and refused to say anything at all about it except that, when he gave me the tape, he admitted that he had been paralysed by the whole horror until Arnison looked around. Then only one concept was in his mind: sanctuary. He was found, of course, quite catatonic, clutching the knocker on the north door.

The drownings

The Solway Firth is well known for its mists: low clouds gather over the rounded hills of Galloway, sea frets come as the tides cover the long moving sands, and the smoke from coal-fires thickens the mists to yellow fog. An entirely clear day is a rarity, but the sun, when it comes, disperses most hazes. On that late summer day the mist still hung well after noon, a vapour more sinister than any generated by sea or sun.

It rose from damp thatch smouldering, smoke twisting from the dying fires of the poor possessions heaped on the green, from excited horses steaming, and most horribly from the gaping bellies and severed limbs of tormented bodies. A score of these were scattered amongst the sacked village, some ripped open, others cut about until hardly recognizable, some clothed, some naked, and one in black decapitated, the head stuck on a pitchfork's prongs. Some crows had gathered, waiting, and dogs were lurking, distress and hunger fighting in them for predominance.

They were waiting for the men to go. A troop of dragoons, bright in scarlet and blue but stained with blood and soot, white-faced or red with excitement as their natures took them, had gathered the surviving women and children together. Their captain, a tall, brutishly handsome man, inspected the captives. He indicated two, one a stout neatly dressed woman in her fifties, set and angry beyond measure, the other a pale fair girl clad in white, not yet in her twenties.

'Mount up and bring them along. Let the others whine psalms over their dead, for it'll take a lot of praying to bring them back to life.' His voice was thick with tension, and carried a strangely out-of-place quality. As he placed his left hand on the sheepskin saddlecloth, the captain saw with disgust that is was red with blood. 'God's teeth, throw me a cloth!'

One of the troopers holding the women grinned, and ripped the white skirt off the girl. 'This'll do for ye, capt'n.' The girl, now suddenly naked from the waist down, shrank into the arms of the older woman, who covered her with her own capacious garments.

'Oh cut, for Christ sake cut!' An angry man in a University of Nebraska T-shirt and elegantly faded jeans emerged from behind the cameras. 'You're meant to be a band of brutal and licentious soldiery, not a Monty Python sketch. And it's the seventeenth fornicating century. You there on the grey, you're riding with your knees round your navel. Lengthen your leathers. Mike, you're meant to be a gentleman: the word is pronounced cloth, not clorf. And Lavvy, dearest, stand still for a second when he rips the skirt off. It's meant to be a shock, not something that happens twice nightly with a matinee on Saturday. We're all going to have to put in a lot more work on this before it's right, but I've had enough for today.'

The props and continuity girls started their rounds, removing the plastic innards and blood, while the liberated corpses blinked and stretched themselves. One unfortunate corpse had real pig's entrails distributed over his person in order to achieve the authentic steaming effect. The severed head was given a light dusting with a sable brush and packed carefully in its own box. Everyone, although relieved that the day's work was done, was sulky in varying degrees. As usual, Sparks grumbled loudest, supported by the grips, but all agreed that it wasn't quite as bad as Felix made out, and all the company knew very well what was really bugging him.

Brian, the chief cameraman, fearsomely ugly, with near-terminal acne and the last man in the industry to use Brylcreem, but whose professional talents had brought him to the top of his trade, took the irate director aside. 'Look, Felix, I'd go a bit easy if I were you. We've only budgeted for ten days here, and we won't do it at this rate. I know they're not the best, but they're all we've got, and they don't improve by nagging. Lute's going to be here this weekend, and he'll want to see things pretty well sewn up.'

Felix looked at the end of his nose. Assistant directors, even when doing all the real work for such a well-known absentee director as Luther Kinsella, who regarded his time as better spent in the Carlyle or the Connaught hobnobbing with producers and the press rather than enduring the discomforts of location, are not all that much higher in the pecking-order than first-class cameramen. Especially when they have reached their forties with no great tang of commercial success about them. But honestly, the actors were as wooden as a lot of peg dolls, and that bloody Mike sounded more like a Hackney con-man than a captain of horse. Nevertheless, there was no point in simply being beastly: it was time to take some action that would teach somebody a very necessary lesson. So Felix nodded, and punched Brian lightly on the arm in what he knew would be accepted as a gesture of affection.

He turned to the dispersing company. 'All right, boys and girls, and horses. Sorry I was a bit sharp then, but it doesn't look quite right from here. Still, we've got a lot in the can that'll be really good, and tomorrow morning we'll just sharpen up that last scene a bit. Brian's got some ideas on lighting that may help. Then we'll get down to drowning Lavvy and Sid, and be back in town on Tuesday as arranged.'

Mollified, the cast and crew continued changing and packing before returning to their hotels in and around Kirkcudbright. The film was being shot in Galloway because Luther liked authenticity, if he did not have to incommode himself unduly, and the story of the drownings was very much a Galloway tale, founded on the facts of history.

After the Restoration in 1660 a triumphant Church of England had tried to bring the recalcitrant Scots round to their way of thinking. They were completely unsuccessful: the Scots had become dourly and tenaciously Presbyterian and resisted the intrusion of what they saw as Popery with the Solemn League and Covenant. Ultimately they were successful and the State Church in Scotland became Presbyterian, with the interesting result that the Queen changes her faith every time she passes through Berwick. But at that time the Covenanters, hounded by Royal cavalry, were fighting a bitter guerilla war in the hills of Galloway, using the weapons and methods they had grown accustomed to in those centuries of Border fighting that had only come to a partial end with the Union of the Crowns.

Some of the Royalist commanders were bloody and cruel even by the standards of the time, and many atrocities were perpetrated, among the best-known of which was the killing of two women, Meg Wilson and Margaret M'Lauchlan. They had been accused of helping the Covenanters, and were tied to stakes in the Solway at low water, to be slowly drowned in the rising tide.

The film used this incident as the beginning of a revenge drama that was described by the producer as a 'tartan Western', ignoring the fact that anyone wearing a tartan in the Lowlands of seventeenth-century Scotland would have been shot on sight by dragoons and Covenanters alike.

Felix could be relied upon to sort out this sort of historical detail; he had the reputation of being a good workmanlike director of films which the critics were not too unkind about and which were reasonably well paid for by television companies. It was not the reputation he would have wished, but, at forty-five, it was that with which he must be content.

In the ordinary course of things the film-making should have gone well enough. There were no great acting names to make difficulties, apart from those playing the two cameo roles of Charles II and the Duchess of Richmond, who took one-third of the casting budget for three minutes of screen time but whose names looked good on the publicity. Ten days of location work should give a good footage to play with, and the rest could be shot comfortably in the studio. That things were not going according to plan was Felix's fault: he stood in danger of committing the unpardonable sin of allowing personal relations to affect the film. He was in love.

Two years previously he had met a girl straight out of drama school with the unlikely name of Lavinia Smith. A sparkling affair had quickly followed: jaded after twenty years in films, Felix felt a new world opening before him, capable of anything with the stimulus of Lavinia.

She however became if not bored, at least ready for something else, and slowly drifted away from Felix's increasing possessiveness. She was a quiet, self-contained girl of considerable strength of character, determined to do well in her profession. Had she been moved only by self-interest she might have been thought unpleasantly calculating, but she followed her emotional inclinations with the same calm determination that she brought to her career.

She had been genuinely in love with Felix, and was now equally genuinely tired of him. Their affair had certainly helped her professionally – she owed this, her first important role, to it – but she would have brought it to an end when she did even if her prospects might have been damaged, being incapable of that particular dishonesty. Felix might have coped better with her leaving had she not decided to take up with Mike Morley, the actor playing the dragoon captain. Mike had much to condemn him in Felix's eyes: he was young and an actor (both unforgivable), nearly illiterate (Harrow and RADA) and persisted in carrying his painstakingly cultivated Cockney accent into quite unsuitable parts. Worst of all, for Felix took films seriously, he would never be more than passably good, while Lavinia had it in her to be very good indeed.

Lavinia had sensibly accepted the need to prevent tensions worsening, and was keeping apart from Mike until the film was made: if she had not, Felix would certainly have precipitated some unpleasantness, but she did not disguise her resolution and rejected any move from Felix for a reconciliation. Her calmness had only served to infuriate Felix: his life had been ruined, but she was as cool as ever, quite happy to continue in as affable a fashion as might suit him, so that when Felix brought some ice and tonic to her room that evening – he knew she kept a hospitable bottle of gin – she accepted the drink he produced and went on with her preparations as she would have done when they were lovers.

Felix had been guilty of a petty piece of spite in ensuring that Lavinia was not given a bathroom: there were some, but not many, in the hotel, and he had not seen why she should not be one of those to suffer a little. It was perhaps revenge on her part that Lavinia was now so openly using the wash-hand basin for purposes for which it was never intended. She was a small, elegantly shaped girl, with a pale and understated colour. In a party she might pass unnoticed, and was often happy to do so, but naked, soaping herself abstractedly, she looked ravishingly desirable. Felix handed her a towel and saw from a pack on the dressing-table that she was back on the pill. His heart hardened: it was time she learned something about other people's feelings. Well, he had worked out something that would shake her up a little.

'Look, love, I'm sorry if I got a bit tetchy today. It's really going well enough, and you're doing quite splendidly.' The episode with the skirt had been another attempted bit of humiliation by Felix, and her quiet acceptance of it had exacerbated his anger and his determination to extract some sort of emotional reaction from her.

'I know the script isn't all that hot, and Lute's no Bertolucci, but this is going to be a bit more than a run-of-the-mill production. It's a new concept, and might start a fashion – like those Dollar epics, but nowhere near as bad. What it will do is look absolutely smashing. The landscape and the light is extraordinary, and we can do some great things.'

'It's a wonderful spot,' said Lavinia, shaking talcum powder over herself, 'a sort of understated sea with no breakers or rocks, and lots of subtle mists.'

'You haven't heard the score yet. It's one of Bruno's best, especially for the climax: his woodwind is extraordinary. The last bit, the drowning, is going to be a runaway success. They'll never have seen anything like it before. Brian is very excited about the camera work – your hair, the waves – it'll be a succession of images – the stills will be in all the books. And look, Lavinia, I want to make a really good thing of it, to celebrate our time together, you know. I'd like it to rest as a sort of tribute to all the good times we've shared. They're over now, but they were good while they lasted.'

Lavinia was as touched as she had it in her to be. 'That's jolly nice of you, Felix: they *were* good times, weren't they? Just pass those knickers would you?'

Felix mentally ground his teeth: he'd show that constipated little slut. They had another gin and went down to dinner together, sharing a bottle of the hotel's frozen Chablis. The cast, feeling that this all portended trouble, kept their distance, and Felix was able to pursue his plot. To make sure of the absolute perfection of the drowning scene he'd like to have a look at the shore as the sun set that evening. He could visualize it all – her hair, pale as the sands, the livid clouds – a summation of the whole story in a single shot, avoiding all the lurking clichés.

After dinner they walked through the hotel woods, over the dunes to the beach. It was deserted, low tide, great stretches of wet sand, the sea far away, birds hunting in the pools, and the sun setting over the Irish Sea and briefly illuminating the Cumbrian peaks on the southern shore. The two execution posts were already in place, one nearer the waves than the other, for the older woman had been placed so that she had to see the younger girl die first, and to call to her what words of comfort she might while the dragoons jeered from the shore.

The scene was indeed magical, and Lavinia, appreciating that Felix knew his business, was well able to imagine the splendid effects which might be possible. Felix encouraged her to something like enthusiasm and wondered, just for a moment, whether they might start all over again. But he knew better, and pressed on with his project.

43

'I'll just take a few stills while we've got this light – they'll give you an idea of what the film will look like. Lean against the post, will you, love –' Lavinia made no bones about standing against her pillar, and even realistically straining her hands behind it. Felix then, with some dexterity, slipped a looped piece of cord round her thumbs, so that she was effectively unable to move from her position.

'Come off it, darling. I can do it well enough without props.'

Felix stood behind her, and whispered, 'Oh no, Lavinia dear, this is for real. You've never suffered in your life, except when you've eaten too much.' It was true that she was a hearty eater. 'But you can start now. It's just on low tide and you'll have plenty of time to reflect on life, and things. You can try screaming, of course, but the nearest person's half a mile away and drinking hard, if I know them around here.'

Lavinia said nothing: she had been trying to free her thumbs but had only pulled the knot tighter. The human hand, with its opposed thumbs facing the palm, makes it almost impossible to undo such a binding without using the teeth, and this is out of the question when the hands are tied behind. She had to shuffle round the post to face Felix.

'You bastard! All that rot was just an excuse to get me here. You always were a shit. I'll tell everyone just what a shit you are.' Felix moved round again, forcing her to wriggle after him.

'You should hope that I'm not such a shit. Just think, you may not be able to tell anybody anything in a few hours' time. The tide's starting to rise already. You'd better hope that I do come back, hadn't you?'

Lavinia continued to curse him, but he slipped away back up the beach. She was so angry that she could not bring herself to scream. It would only give him the satisfaction of thinking that she was frightened, and she was not. She was sure that he was lurking in the wood, waiting for her to break down.

In this she was mistaken. Felix had procured a copy of the tide tables and worked out the position of Lavinia's post above low water. With that night's tide her head should be about three feet below the surface at high water. A fourteen-foot rise should see the tide around her waist a couple of hours before high water. He would come back then and watch her being really scared, begging to be untied as the water rose, before showing himself. At least then she would know something of what she'd put him through.

He did not want to be seen back at the hotel in case any questions should be asked, so he drove to a small pub a few miles away on the Newton Stewart road. He had been there once before and knew that they kept a catholic selection of malt whiskies. Some time could profitably be spent comparing the relative merits of Speyside and Islay, a question he had never fully settled, while keeping a prudent eye on his watch. After he had sampled a Laphroaig and a Macallan, and was trying a Glenmorangie, some fishermen came into the bar. Rendered more conversable than usual by an interest in the film, and keen for any opportunity to make a little on the side should any boats be needed, they struck up a conversation with him.

They started on the hallowed topic of the weather, and progressed to the fishing and the tides. 'Och, its an uncanny queer place this arld river. There's bays a fush is never seen, and others they'll flock tae, and there's bays full of dangers, and others as safe as a kailyard. It's worse over the Cumberland side, but there's naebody gaes there, but there's some bad bits near here – there's that bay you're at, for one. Some of the queerest tides in the Firth.'

Felix felt a little prickle of apprehension in his neck muscles. 'Oh, and why's that?'

'It's to do with the way the sands run. The tide comes in slow to start, like it does anywhere, and it finishes slow, too. In the middle it moves like a galloping horse. There's many a man been trapped by that, crossing the sands.'

Felix looked at his watch again. It was nearly time for him to be off. He said casually, 'How would the tide be now, would you say?' The man did not need to check the time, for like any having to do with the sea he knew the state of the tide and the direction of the wind at any time. 'Och, nae so far off high water, to be sure, and making slower noo.'

Lavinia could have confirmed the truth of this. She had been working out some method of breaking free, after having given up trying to undo the cord. There was a nail she could just reach, and she had tried rubbing the cord against it. Or it might be possible to climb the post, although very difficult to manage it backwards. She was very cold and fed up, and her arms hurt.

Then the first water started trickling around her feet. She became alarmed, and then, as every wave came a little higher, frightened. At last she started to scream.

Felix, back in the pub, had gone rather pale. His heart, which always gave him trouble at times of stress, started thumping irregularly. He put down his drink and moved quickly to the car. It was only a matter of four miles, but through winding Kirkcudbrightshire lanes. He drove wildly, never out of second gear, taking corners blindly, driving the car over the sands as far as he could, then running and stumbling through the marram grass.

The moon had come out, and showed the beach quite empty. There was no sign of the posts, and the tide was not far from full. Felix tore off his clothes and plunged into the sea. He realized that he had no idea of even the approximate whereabouts of the posts. He swam up and down, round in circles, plunging and groping under the surface of the icy waters, terrified at the thought of what he might find.

He found nothing. Utterly exhausted, he made for the shore: he dared not go back to the hotel or raise the alarm. He sat shivering in the car for what seemed hours, until once more the tops of the posts appeared through the receding water. He waded out: the posts were empty.

He was confused and distraught. If Lavinia had got herself

loose, or been freed, she would have been here by now, kicking up the most enormous row. Had she perhaps floated off with the tide? It was quite possible, for she was not attached to the post, and her drowned body could have moved freely up on the rising water.

His own body began to crave the consolation of warmth and whisky, cigarettes, a hot bath, but when he reached his bedroom, unobserved, he could do nothing but flop exhausted on the bed without even turning on the light.

He lay without moving, then stretched, and groaned. His hand met something beside him on the bed, something wet and cold.

He jumped up, ran to the door, and switched on the light. Lavinia lay on the bed. Seaweed was in her hair and mouth; her eyes stared upwards. The crabs had already been at work: the corners of her mouth and nose were nibbled away. The soft parts of her body, abraded by the post and the shingle, had been further eroded by hungry fish. There was a stench of cold decaying death. The eyes turned slowly towards him.

Felix hung on the half-open door. The paroxysmal beating started again, thundering, and stopped as he collapsed on the floor.

Lavinia got up, wiped off the make-up which she had borrowed for the occasion, removed the seaweed and some very unpleasant last week's fish, and lit a cigarette.

'Well, you bastard, do you want to know what being dead feels like? Do you? . . . For heaven's sake! *Felix . . .*!'

The quay stairs

Walter Robson was undeniably pleased with himself, and not without reason. He was nineteen, healthy, and possessed of an excellent post in the office of the long-established solicitors, Messrs Porson, Jebb and Bentley of St Thomas's Square. His affectionate family lived a convenient fifty miles off in the market town of Wooler, near enough to give support in times of need but not so near as to interfere with his spending his emoluments as he wished, free of parental inhibition. An attentive landlady, Mrs Pattinson of the Leazes, fed him generously: he had, for example, just come from a supper of pea soup and roast pork, the crackling delectably crisp, with apple-and-blackberry pie: the whole certainly no worse than usual in that it had followed his customary punctual payment of the fortnightly rent, a sum modest enough to leave him with twenty-three shillings at his own command for spending over the next two weeks.

Some of this should doubtless be earmarked for a payment to Mr Moses, the tailor, on account of a handsome Otterburn tweed coat with trousers and waistcoat ditto, all with silk braid, but Mr Moses was patient, and even a junior clerk with Messrs Porson, Jebb and Bentley was a person of respectability and some small consequence, such as tailors were delighted to accept as debtors.

And to be young and prosperous in Newcastle upon Tyne was to have the world at your feet. The city had been rich for centuries as the centre of the sea-coal trade which warmed the whole of England. London could not function for more than a few days if its supply of black gold was held up by storm or civil commotion. Hundreds of collier brigs could be found simultaneously sheltering in North Shields, and the passage to the Thames was the most frequented in Europe. To this ancient prosperity had been added wealth created by the new technologies, which had started with George Stephenson's development of the steam locomotive. Tyneside had become the world's repository of the science of engineering: George's son Robert had established the great locomotive and engineering works at Elswick, William Armstrong had invented the quick-firing gun and built an enormous armaments factory at Scotswood, and the shipyards of Swan, Hunter at Wallsend were building warships for the world. There were more ships built on Tyne, Wear and Tees than in the rest of England and North America put together.

Even for a successful young man in a thriving community, Walter was perhaps a little too pleased with himself; his best friends, at least from time to time, found him rather too much of a good thing, perhaps more especially when they were feeling themselves a little under par. On such occasions his consistent and irrepressible liveliness, exuberant good health and high animal spirits were not easy to bear; a man suffering from gout might feel similarly about a Newfoundland puppy – its qualities, although admirable, would better be exhibited elsewhere.

But there was no denying that Walter was an excellent companion, intelligent, amusing, and always ready for a romp, generous with his time and money and original in his view of life. While other young men most often fell in with received ideas and conformed to accepted practices, he enjoyed playing with the fashionable philosophies, turning them inside out or upside-down, to the delectation of the irreverent. Sometimes indeed he went too far, and earned the justified reproofs of his seniors.

On that particular Friday night Walter was in fine fettle. His supper had been followed by a careful toilette; his whiskers had been suitably pomaded and his nails and fingers pumiced clean of the ink that is the bane of the lives of solicitor's clerks. These preparations had taken rather longer than he had allowed, and some degree of haste was needed if he were not to be late for his meeting with his friend Robert Ridley, a clerk with William Brandts, the merchants of Sandgate. Robert was an engaging companion, something of a poet, nervous and temperamental, but with a nice turn of wit, able to make himself agreeable to the young ladies they sometimes met at concerts in the Old Assembly Rooms or at lectures given by the Literary and Philosophical Society.

Tonight however was to be on a less elevated plane: they were to meet at the Royal Albert Hotel on the Quayside and to walk, after some refreshment, up to the Grand Music Hall at Byker where they would almost certainly meet some ladies of a more frivolous sort and jollier mien. It was in such encounters that Walter, more dashing and apter for sociability than his friend, would make the running. He was confident of his abilities in this line, although he could have wished that his moustache would develop a little faster; his whiskers were, as might vulgarly be said, coming on a treat.

He was already in a hurry as he made his way through the crowded Cloth Market: the colourful stalls full, not of the fabrics that had been there during the Middle Ages, but of shining oranges, steaming hot pies, penknives, of sarsparilla and dandelion and burdock for the more temperate, of patent medicines for the afflicted, and pomade and perfume for the dandified, were illuminated by blazing naphtha flares that made the ruddy glistening cheeks of the girls more brilliant than ever. Walter received an encouraging number of lewd suggestions and admiring cries as he ran their gauntlet, and grinned back at the prettier of them, but did not loiter, walking briskly out of the market past the town hall and the cathedral, on to the approach to that masterpiece of the younger Stephenson's, the High Level Bridge which carried both road- and rail-traffic at a considerable elevation over the River Tyne.

Since he was a punctual young man, as befitted a solicitor's clerk, Walter had decided to make use of a short cut that he had not tried before, in order to arrive at the meeting on time. This route necessitated turning sharply off the High Level approach, leaving the bright incandescent gaslights, and entering the purlieus of the ancient castle. The New Castle, built by Henry I and occupying a commanding position on the north bank of the River Tyne, had much decayed from its original magnificence: the huge mouldering relics of the Black Gate, the main entrance, remained, as did the immense gaunt keep, the starkest memorial of Norman military architecture. Besides these, only a few crumbling structures, diverted from their original purpose, served as storehouses and refuges for human and animal wreckage. The whole, in a triumphant affirmation of nineteenth-century materialism, was bisected by the main line of the York–Newcastle and Berwick Railway, whose signals flashed against the black mass of the ruined keep.

Here the lighting, after the bright illuminations of the city centre, was dim and fitful. Walter had to slow down, picking his way over the rutted path that led through the ruins: he could discern a light ahead shining in a gateway, which served as a guide; as he approached the gateway it could be seen to be a postern in the castle's outer wall, which at this point was co-terminous with the more extensive walls of the city, at the very crest of the steep banks of the river. It was not the pleasantest of places; pools of foetid liquid lay about: the stones were black and soft with soot and grime. The light that had led him was a single gas jet without the benefit of an incandescent mantle, served by some defective piping that caused the flame to gutter and flare, sighing with the falling and rising pressure, bringing the dark shadows into momentary illumination.

The young man paused under the gateway to survey his path. Before him a long flight of steep steps ran down to the Quayside; the treads were sunk in darkness until, at the bottom, another gas jet flickered and the lights of the riverside could be seen. To the right of the steps was a high wall topped with broken glass to discourage intruders; on the left, a series of derelict buildings descending in line with the stairs. The smell was atrocious, bringing to mind putrescence and decay. Only the gate itself, crowned with rusty iron spikes, and the nearest building, were at all clearly visible.

That edifice might have been either a house or a warehouse, but it had been abandoned for some time; the single door and the windows were boarded, the black walls streaked with green where rainwater had flowed down broken drains. In spite of the unprepossessing surroundings Walter was not too taken with the idea of descending the steps; from what he could see they looked uncommonly worn and slippery, nor did he feel inclined to risk his new kid gloves on the filthy handrail. He was indeed much inclined to turn back and reach the Quayside by a more conventional route.

As he hesitated he looked at the house more closely; the door was certainly secured by three substantial planks, nailed horizontally across, but, unless it was a trick of the gas, one plank seemed to move slightly; he went a little nearer and could hear something, an odd noise like a rat scratching, but not as an animal might scratch, flurried and irregular. This scratching was a steady, persistent abrasion, neither loud nor heavy, but untiring and insistent, and was caused by a larger nail or claw than that of a small rodent. As he watched and listened, the scratching proved its efficacy. The topmost of the securing boards made a perceptible move, and the whole door creaked softly as if loosening its structure.

Suddenly the idea of the steps became much more acceptable; whatever was behind that door was trying to get out, and Walter did not want to stay upon the success of its attempts. Heedless of the damage to his gloves, he bounded down the stairs towards the lights below.

At the foot of the steps, which he gained in a very short space of time, he recovered himself almost immediately; he was a resilient young man and ashamed of the panic that had momentarily overcome him. Arrived at the Royal Albert, with the companionable noise and warmth of the tavern around him and his very dirty gloves stuffed in a pocket, he was quite able to make a joke of nearly having fallen down the stairs. Young Ridley was, however, a little put out. 'You would do well to avoid that neighbourhood, old lad. It's got a bad reputation on the Quayside; far too convenient for all sorts of mischief. There've been some nasty things happen there, and the results quietly slipped in the river.'

Walter was dismissive. 'Oh come, Robert, this is the nineteenth century! The days of Gothick horrors are done with; ghouls and footpads have fled before gaslights and the police force, even down here on your old Quayside. Let's go and find some girls at the Grand.'

Robert had to admit that no incidents of a sinister nature had taken place there in recent years, but insisted that the stairs were best avoided; for his part, Walter was content to agree on their decayed nature as representing a hazard, and they left in time for the second house at the music hall.

For some time after this incident things continued to go well for Walter. He progressed in the good opinion of Mr Charles Bentley, the junior partner of the firm, to whom the young clerk was chiefly responsible. Perhaps he had lost something of his earlier tendency to frolic, but this was probably just a natural result of growing older. Any disagreeable thoughts were thrust to the back of his mind, and it was only occasionally, in the watches of the night, that the noise of that rasping came back to him. Was it imagination, or had something really been there behind the door? And if so, what could it have been? There was a temptation to see for himself, but this he managed to resist, and, with time, the wish to do so receded. For reasons of ordinary prudence he avoided the stairs on future expeditions, and stuck to the more usual approach to the Quayside by way of Grey Street. Only once did anything happen to recall that unpleasant episode.

As a general rule the excursions he made with Robert Ridley and his other friends were of the more conventional sort.

53

Newcastle at that time was, as befitted the richest town in the country, a centre for visiting celebrities, and the theatres and concerts attracted the most famous artists. The wages of Walter and his friends could only run to the milder dissipations, and indeed they were not greatly tempted to stray from the paths of rectitude. It was one of Robert's seafaring friends, a junior officer with the flourishing Runciman fleet, who introduced them to their only foray into the underworld.

For this it was necessary to move further afield; the city fathers kept a tight hand on goings-on, and the Newcastle police force was not an institution that the criminal classes were anxious to cross. South Shields, a few miles away in the County of Durham, was altogether an easier-going place, with a plentiful supply of seamen's taverns and other even less respectable institutions. Walter and Robert drew the line at some of these, but did agree to visit what their friend told them was a Chinese eating-house. Robert was rather taken by this, and fell to quoting Mr Tennyson's popular lines on Ulysses; Walter was convinced, from the strange odours and the soporific appearance of the clientele, that worse things than food were available.

He was dealing as best he might with chopsticks when he became aware of the noise, a quiet, persistent scratching: he turned towards the source and saw an old Chinaman in a blue silk robe. The fingernails on his right hand were horribly long, protruding inches beyond the tips of the fingers, and were scratching at a spot on the blue silk. Walter shivered; the Chinaman smiled; and the noise stopped. It was nothing – but the idea of those nails, linked with the much more powerful activity that he had heard by the stairs, gave him a most unwelcome impression of what might have been there, behind that door. Sleep did not come easily that night as he lay awake, listening, conscious of all the small noises that surrounded him: he left the gas mantle burning until the sound of it reminded him of that other light, when he quickly turned it off.

Had it not been for this incident, and the need Walter felt to reassert his nerve, it is likely that he might have forgotten about the whole thing, and not have been tempted into the next unfortunate episode.

It was not long afterwards that one of those minor crises that occur in the business world cropped up. Young Ridley's firm did much business with Russia, importing timber, cordage, tar, and other marine items, and lading the returning vessels, whenever possible, with English manufactures. Walter's senior partner, old Mr Porson, served as the Russian Imperial consul in Newcastle, and it was indeed in this connection that the two young men had first met. On this occasion a valuable consignment of locomotive spares and equipment was being shipped from Stephenson's factory: since it was an official cargo, fulfilling an order placed by a department of the Russian government, the bills of lading had to be countersigned by the consul. There had been some delay in their preparation, and Walter, who had been given the responsibility for progressing the transaction, had been kept waiting at the works.

By the time he had collected the bills and taken them to his firm's chambers, time was running out if the tide was to serve. Old Mr Porson did his part as expeditiously as possible, but when all the work was complete Walter found himself pressed for time. The ship, already laden, was lying at the town quay, just downstream of the High Level Bridge, and Walter determined to take the route down the stairs, which was certainly the most direct.

He was hard put to explain this course of conduct to himself; perhaps the official nature of his business, and the imposing documents which he carried in a handsome morocco portfolio, lent him a certain courage; perhaps, too, the sleepless nights he had passed had given him a certain desperation; the thing must be faced, and if boldly faced, might prove to be nothing. Before he had much leisure to consider the matter he found himself again approaching the ruined gate, the house and the stairs.

It was all as he recalled it; the smell, if anything, was worse.

He had intended to walk quickly past but, unable to take his eyes from the door, he slowed his pace, and halted. One of the planks had indeed fallen, and there were but two remaining to secure the door. Where the fallen plank had been there was a long groove in the wood of the door. Even as he watched he saw the second plank move, a slight twitch, and heard again the terrible, persistent, powerful, intent scratching. The disgusting foetid stench grew stronger.

His rush down the steps, tearing himself away, was made in blank terror, and when he got himself across the quay and on board the ship, into the warmth of the master's cabin, he was shaking uncontrollably. The captain was a humane man, much struck by Walter's evident distress, and in spite of his anxiety about the tide, pressed a glass of gin and water on him, a remedy in which he had the greatest faith.

Sitting in the small day cabin, panelled in mahogany, lit by gimballed lights, warmed by steam pipes, and soothed by the gentle motion of the river, Walter found that the restorative did its work, as did the comfort of human proximity. Walter was a descendent of generations of Border farmers, and Border raiders before that, men not noted for the nervousness of their dispositions; and as he walked home, keeping to the well lit and populated thoroughfares, he determined to cast off the weight from his mind.

Unfortunately on attempting to sleep that night, he met with great difficulty, and had recourse to ten drops of laudanum that his landlady kept for such emergencies. After a troubled sleep he awoke in a high fever, screaming.

The doctor diagnosed brain fever brought on by over-work, and prescribed a low diet and cupping. This proved an excellent treatment, as the discomfort of the blood-letting produced a determination to recover, and in a week he was on his legs and doing well. Mr Charles was sufficiently concerned to pay him a visit, bearing gratifyingly friendly messages from the senior partners and insisting that Walter should take leave of absence, paid for one week, in order to feel the benefits of a convalescent holiday. Accordingly, Walter spent that time in the bosom of his family and in the bracing air of the Northumbrian country-side.

To no one, family, friends or colleagues, did he mention his experience on the steps or the strange door outside the walls.

On his return to the office, however, he determined to find out what he could of the whole history of that sinister place. The very next day he set about his task, finding some pretext to visit the town archives; previous experience in searching for property titles had given him some knowledge of the unsystematic arrangements there, and he was soon able to collect a fair amount of information. Terriers and plans were available back to the sixteenth century, and there were some indentures prior to that date. From these it seemed as though the area between the city walls and the Quayside had always been something of a no-man's-land. Properties had been erected without any very clear titles and had been used indifferently as warehouses, lodging houses, taverns, and worse. Since it was outside the city walls, the rule of the city fathers did not run, and the sheriff of the county did not bother with the affairs of the small enclave. The rapidly changing population of the place had resisted any attempts that might have been made to control it, and the authorities washed their hands of whatever might go on there.

And some very peculiar things had gone on. The earliest records showed the area was used for plague pits and the burials of executed criminals: the heads of malefactors had been exposed on the gate, together with those parts of the anatomies of criminals sentenced to hanging, drawing and quartering that had been allocated to the City of Newcastle. Judicial amputations and castrations had been carried out and the detritus of all these proceedings dumped on the waste land. In later years, for which Walter had resort to cuttings from local newspapers, after the area had been built over, the place became a recognized haunt of the villainous, and the focus of many horrible crimes.

With the improvements of the nineteenth century, and a

more humane and liberal attitude, most of the area's inhabitants found their way to the new asylums for the insane or to houses of correction, and the buildings that had been the scene of so much violence and vice were abandoned.

Walter found himself comforted by these researches; it seemed reasonable that a place which had for centuries seen so much wickedness might quite well retain some noxious and evil influences. He did not intend to speculate whether these might have some corporeal manifestation and, left to himself, would have made every effort to put the whole thing from his mind and resume his comfortable existence. At all costs he would avoid going near that terrible place again; he went so far as to consider leaving the city. It would not have been too difficult to obtain a situation elsewhere but he was reluctant to do so, although never clear as to his reasons. The force of human inertia is considerable; peasants cling to their farms, trusting that the volcano will not erupt during their own lifetimes, and Indian villagers continue to till their fields while a tiger lurks in the undergrowth.

Man is rarely, however, left to himself, and Walter was no exception; with the most innocent of motives, but the most fatal of consequences, Robert Ridley took a hand. Robert had attributed the change in his friend's behaviour after his illness, as he became more studious and less lively, to that most common of maladies, love. At first this amused him, and he teased Walter about his supposed passion, and speculated as to its object: when this produced no elucidation, Robert was inclined to sulk, believing his friend reluctant to confide in him. Walter, divining the cause, and being unwilling to occasion unhappiness, felt it necessary to tell young Ridley something of the story.

Being a poet, Ridley was naturally curious and did his best to draw out Walter on the detail of the incident, for Walter had told it in the most general terms and had persisted in refusing to name the place. Robert pursued the topic with some cunning, refraining from direct questioning but essaying little conjectures from time to time which served to eliminate one spot after another, without allowing Walter to suspect how much he had, in fact, revealed.

This curiosity was spurred by a deep distaste on Ridley's part for anything that might be termed superstitious or supernatural: he came from a Unitarian family and was a fervent rationalist, following Shelley in looking on all forms of religion with scorn and on such things as ghosts and warlocks with contempt. On these grounds he determined to save Walter from what he knew to be demented delusions which, if unchecked, might lead to permanent derangement, by exposing the baselessness of his apprehensions. In much the same way he would have acted had his friend showed signs of Popery or even Puseyism.

Ridley was confirmed in his suspicions that he had discovered the truth about the location of the incidents on observing Walter's attempts at prevarication when a meeting at the Royal Albert was suggested: he remembered the first occasion, and the dirty gloves, and the route that had been chosen. Accordingly he decided to investigate the very next Saturday, before their customary rendezvous which, bowing to Walter's wishes, had instead been fixed for Robinson's Wine Cellars in the Cloth Market, a safe distance from the castle and the quay.

That evening Walter was present on time at Robinson's, helped himself to a generous pinch of the snuff provided by the house, ordered a large glass of marsala, and settled down to an examination of the *Evening Chronicle*. It was at the time of the exciting events in Sicily, which was the reason he had ordered that wine as a tribute to the great dictator of that island, who had landed with his immortal Thousand at that very port. The despatch was so absorbing that it was some time before he realized the absence of his friend, normally the soul of punctuality. What was even stranger was that there had been no message: Newcastle was rich in small boys who could be trusted, for one penny down and another on safe arrival, to deliver messages to all parts of the city.

A suspicion formed in his mind; he finished the marsala and hurried off to Robert's lodgings, not far off in the Westgate Road. As he walked his concern grew; Robert had been persistently curious of late, and it might be that he had let slip more than he thought. If Robert had attempted to investigate on his own, the results might be unimaginable. The old horrors returned, and it was a pallid and shaking young man who had his worst fears confirmed by Robert's landlady: her lodger had indeed left, well over an hour before, after borrowing a lantern and a crowbar, about which she had teased him, suggesting he was about to begin a career of crime.

For a moment Walter was incapable of coherent thought; every instinct rebelled against the prospect of that fearful place, the wavering light, the stench, and the restless thing within. It was the bravest of actions that he took when he turned from the landlady's door and ran as fast as he was able through the streets to the castle.

As often happens, action clears the mind, and in his wild dash, which excited the attention of many, Walter forgot most of the oppression that had weighed upon him. When he reached the arch with the gas flame, the whole place seemed curiously changed. The flame burnt steadily, the pools seemed smaller, the stench had gone; the crumbling gaunt building was just an old and dirty house. But the door, bereft of its supporting planks, now hung ajar and askew from a single hinge, quite open. On the threshold lay a crowbar.

By this time a policeman, followed by some spectators, had caught up with Walter, who was too much out of breath to be able to explain matters; he merely indicated the door and the crowbar. In truth, in spite of the access of courage that had brought him there, nothing would have induced him to enter the house. The change that seemed to have taken place only convinced him that something very terrible had happened; whatever had been within, confined and restless, was now free, and, he was quite sure, sated.

The policeman did not venture far, for the whole edifice was so rotten and crumbling as to make any entrance perilous, but, having sent for assistance, stood on duty to prevent anyone else risking their necks. Within a very few minutes men arrived equipped with ropes, planks and lanterns. There could be no question of a speedy entry: the men had to work very carefully, laying the planks across gaps in the floor, edging foot by foot into the dark interior.

Walter, torn between fear and concern, followed not too closely behind them. The lanterns disclosed heaps of unidentifiable putrescent matter, and quantities of filth and cobwebs disturbed in places as though some large animal had made a lair. As the men moved forward the light penetrated further into the dark corners. Walter glanced instinctively after it, and quickly looked away, his throat and mouth dry. He thought – he was almost sure – he had seen a movement there in the mounds of rubble. A movement like that of some amorphous beast sidling back into the shadows. And there had been a flicker of light on something hard and shining, as of bone, fang or claw. Walter stayed no longer but stumbled, retching, back into the air.

The men emerged after a few more minutes to report no sign of life. They had however found in one room, where the floorboards had rotted away completely, a deep hole or well which appeared to contain semi-liquid material. Since any exploration in that dim light would have been extremely risky, the investigation was postponed until the following morning, and the door left temporarily blocked and under the guard of a constable.

When the search resumed in daylight nothing more was discovered, and of Robert there was no trace at all. It was thought that he must have either fallen into the well or become the victim of a shanghai-ing captain, an occurrence that was not unknown. Walter had his own theories, which he kept to himself. There might not have been anything moving in the shadows, but he knew that he had imagined neither the scratching nor the movement he had seen on the door.

It was agreed that the house was dangerous and should be destroyed, the well being filled with rubble. Walter later used his influence with the authorities, which grew as he prospered, to have a stout iron plate fixed over what had been the well: it was good to be sure about these things, and indeed the place has remained safe to this day. Even the best iron rusts, however, and after more than a century the cover has grown frail. It is to be hoped that due prudence will be observed in any building operations that might take place near the old walls of New-castle, and that the city fathers will hold in mind the old tag: '*Quietus non movere.*'

The gibbet

The minibus came to an uncertain halt outside the ferry terminal, the engine stalling as it did so, straddling the white lines which demarcated a space reserved for the cars of customs officers. It was a disreputable and battered vehicle, spattered with accretions of mud and slurry, bearing the marks of some years of careless and inexpert handling. The men who stumbled out, shouting and clutching at each other for support, matched it aptly enough. Bunched together they staggered towards the police checkpoint.

The RUC men, clean and closely shaved, looked at them with disgust. 'Come along there, sort yourselves out. Are you all coming aboard, or are you out for a day by the seaside?' The accent, as well as the neatly pressed uniform and shining boots, marked the officer as a Protestant, and what else would you expect? Wasn't it always a Prod in the uniform ordering decent men about? No, it was only the one, Stephen, God save the lad, going to his fine job in Glasgow. The others were just there to give him a proper send-off.

Stephen, pale and unsteady, was holding his tickets crumpled into a damp mess. The Special Branch man standing behind the uniformed constable looked at him closely. The description could fit: the moustache might have been removed, and the long hair cut. He moved forward, touching the policeman's sleeve, but as he did so one of the drunks doubled up, retching, and was violently sick. Vomit splashed everywhere but chiefly on the trousers and boots of the RUC man, who drew back with an exclamation of disgust – bloody Taigues, drunken and irresponsible louts!

The Special Branch man, who had avoided the uprush, smiled. It was hardly likely that this impossible collection of soaks could be consorting with highly competent professionals. The description, such as it was, fitted thousands of others as well: it was not worth while investigating. He turned away, letting Stephen climb aboard and the policeman none too gently pushed his repellent companions back on to the quay.

Once on board, Stephen made his way to the forward bar and collapsed on to a bench. No attention was paid to so common a sight as a drunken Irishman sleeping it off on the way to Stranraer, and he was left undisturbed.

He was far from sleep, however. Christ, that was a brilliant move of Sean's. The plain-clothes man had noticed something, he was sure. But suddenly being sick all over the bastards! That was the ideal block. Just another batch of drunken peasants: he could see the derision pass beyond their eyes.

It had been a good operation, all things considered: the staffwork had been first class. The driver and Maire had rehearsed the whole thing time after time back there in the south, while the lads up here had watched every movement the Governor had made in the last three weeks, without ever a suspicion being raised. Although the screw had been careful not to establish a pattern, as the rules of security prescribed, discernible sequences had emerged. Somehow or other a complete plan of the house had been obtained, with every piece of furniture marked, so that when the woman had opened the door to Maire – and Jesus Mary! hadn't she looked innocent and helpless, hands dirtied by ineffectually trying to change the wheel, a silly pretty girl if there ever was one – he had been able to dash inside, into the living-room, knowing exactly where everything would be, and where the Governor would be sitting, gin in hand, catching the local news on television.

He had made his own preparations, as well. The pistol, now disposed of in a convenient bog, had been meticulously cleaned; each round had been wiped free of grease – jamming

64

was always a potential hazard with automatics. He had fired several magazines up on the hill and knew the piece's little characteristics. Not that accuracy was a problem; he was an impeccable shot with rifle or handgun, and at ten feet he could hardly be expected to miss.

It had been stupid of the woman to grab the kid. If she had left it on the floor where it had been crawling about it would have lived, but clutching it to her chest, what could she expect? Two .45 slugs had almost fused the bodies together. The Governor had reached for the pistol on the table, but was accounted for by a single neat shot in the face. Maire had looked a bit white, but she was experienced and kept her head. And all that was less than two hours ago. The ports had immediately been inundated with police, but with no reliable description – he'd seen to that – the stupid buggers had crossed him off as only another drunken mick.

The adrenalin stimulated by the shooting and escape was still surging through his system: he could feel his pulse hammering. Sleep was out of the question, although he knew he needed rest since he had not closed his eyes for thirty hours or so. He curled up smugly and thought about previous operations: all had been successful, but some had brought greater satisfaction than others. Rifles were all very well – he had done some good work with the Armalite – but you never really saw the results. Squeeze the trigger, mark the fall, then a dash off to safe cover – whereas with a hand-gun you were face to face, could see the impact, the moment of shock, you were a god, changing the world, bringing blood, death and destruction into a snug well-ordered existence.

Disembarking was tricky, for the police were on their guard: they knew now what had happened on Newtownards and they were looking at everyone with angry suspicion. He was on his own, too; he could rely on no support this time. But he had, as he always had, a plan; during the voyage he had managed to be sick and the vomit on his jacket, the bottle of Old Bushmills sticking from his pocket, his pale face with pink eyes, and his careful, painful walk, were confirmation that he was in the grip of an acute hangover.

Two men were questioning disembarking passengers. One, a uniformed sergeant, was suspicious, checking every face against an identikit photograph: the other, almost equally uniform in his tweed jacket and highly polished shoes, sneered at the stumbling, dishevelled man . . . obviously a bloody bog-trotting Taigue, but never, in any policeman's imagination, a cold-blooded and experienced killer.

They let him through the barriers with a scorn that made him inwardly furious – superior bastards, if only they knew, they would treat him very differently. No sign of this resentment was allowed to show as he shambled off towards the car-park. It was there, as arranged, unremarkable, a blue Fiesta, its keys taped to the nearside front wheel.

As he drove out of the car-park he felt that he could, for the first time in days, afford some relaxation of tension. Once out of Stranraer there should be no major difficulties, but with the usual foresight that planning command showed, a circuitous route had been prepared for him and left in the car, together with maps and a couple of chocolate bars. He ate these immediately, for, neither smoking nor drinking, he needed the sugary jolt to help restore his balance.

On leaving the town he turned off the main road, and, avoiding the popular coast route made his way through Cairn Edward forest and the Forest of Ae to Eskdale and Liddlesdale, well away from the towns of Dumfries and Lockerbie. As he left the gentle green hills of Galloway and came to the slopes of Teviot the landscape changed. The pale winter's sun gave place to liver-coloured sky merging into a cold and dark night. Even at the moderate speeds that were the best that could be managed on the poor roads, he could feel the rising wind shift the car as it moved from the lee of a hill to the unprotected valley.

Navigation grew more difficult: the headlights were ineffective against the gloom and rain, which came in torrential blasts. He made some mistakes, and had to turn on the narrow lanes as best he could, so that when eventually he found the last junction, Saughtree, which would take him straight from Kielder to Newcastle, some fifty miles or so, he was much relieved. It was a nasty spot, too, just on the exposed watershed that forms the Border at that place. On his right Foulmire Heights and Black Knowe loomed up, and ahead were the sharper contours of Carlin Tooth and Peel Waste, only occasionally silhouetted as the clouds admitted a near-full moon. In the old times these had been the Debatable Lands where no honest man settled, where neither English nor Scottish law ran, the last refuge of both kingdoms' felons. Here the old Border families, Eliots and Robsons, Ridleys and Kers, Liddels and Scotts, had fought out their differences and marked every shaw and hillside with violence.

Stephen had only made a couple of miles on the south-bound road when he felt the power failing, and pumped angrily at the accelerator: uselessly, for the engine cut out and the car rolled to a stop. Repeated efforts to restart it produced no response. An electrical fault, perhaps caused by the driving rain flooding the distributor cap? He was damned if he was going to try finding it in this weather, and besides, bending over an open bonnet was an invitation to any well-meaning idiot to stop and offer help. Anyway, he could see a light by the roadside not too far ahead, which could surely only come from a telephone box. He'd get those idle sods in Newcastle away from their dry firesides. It was time somebody this side of the water did something for a change.

When he got out of the car the full force of the wind became apparent as it tore round the bare hillside and funnelled down the dip where the road ran. It was very cold, and the rain was flung horizontally by the gusts.

Pulling his thin anorak about him he climbed from the car and launched himself on to the road. Jesus, it was a terrible night! On every side the bare moors, too wild and barren for even the simplest farming, were empty of any habitation, but the light ahead promised some human contact.

Black though it was, the road was just a little lighter than the moor. There was no fence, but white stones marked the verge and tall striped poles showed how high the snow drifted in the wintertime, so it was not too difficult, in spite of the wind and driving rain, to follow the road towards the light. As he neared the light he saw a taller and more solid post, towering up with a cross-beam at the top, suddenly appear by the roadside, caught in the glow of what he was now able to see to be indeed a GPO telephone box. This symbol of civilization seemed a good omen, welcome in this God-forsaken spot. He hoped some vandal hadn't smashed it. You never could tell with people nowadays.

It seemed that the only trees in the region were clustered round the telephone box, whipped by the wind but providing some protection. Nevertheless he was glad to get into the little lighted space and let the heavy door shut out the wet dark. There had been no vandals, and the Newcastle number he had been given answered, as was the custom, on the tenth ring. Answered, as again was the custom, without speaking to him.

'Look, Tourist' – his code name – 'here. That bloody car's given up. It's the storm; come and get me. I'm just off the B6357 at –' he looked at the information note on the kiosk, 'somewhere called Deadwater Gibbet. It's a bloody awful night. I'm near the telephone, so you'll find me easy enough. Right?'

It was only when he had finished that the voice at the other end responded, 'Right, lad, don't fret, we'll be there within two hours.'

Putting down the telephone, he felt a curious disinclination to move, or even to look around, and continued to stare at his reflection in the glass covering the notices. It was far too public there, and he should get back to the car, but for some reason he was deeply reluctant to look out of the box into the night. The telephone kiosks designed by Sir Giles Gilbert Scott are substantial constructions, but are fully glazed on three sides. The light within shines out freely, and illuminates whatever may be outside. He was suddenly sure, with a sickening certainty that dried his mouth, that anything that might be there outside would be something that should not be seen, much less encountered.

Of course there could be nothing outside, only the wind, and the branches of the trees reaching out, tormented by the gale, black leaves flaking off, driven against the glass.

There could be nothing outside, but he could not even glance to make sure. Trying to concentrate, he looked at the dialling codes on the panel in front of him – *Alnwick, Amble, Ashington* – but his eyes were insistently drawn to the small square where was printed, '*This telephone is situated near the junction of the B6357 at Deadwater Gibbet.*'

Christ, that was it! That black post he had passed must have been the gibbet. In that wild land the gallows could rarely have been empty: the careers of countless evil and violent men had ended on it, their distorted bodies covered in tar, bound with iron straps and chains to keep the slowly decaying flesh together until the black limbs fell apart, the dry flesh flaking off to expose the white bone, falling to the ground, scattered like leaves in the wind.

He was seized by an overwhelming terror that obliterated and annulled normal rational behaviour. Now he understood why he dared not look out at what the light might reveal. And why he must, whatever happened, stay safe inside his small capsule of light in a vast space of dark shadows. They were waiting out there, men of blood like himself who had made pain and terror their pride, ready to welcome him, one of their number. There was one difference – they had paid the penalty for their crimes many years ago out there on the gibbet, while he had escaped, at least until now. The smallest branches of the trees were dashed into the light, receded into the shadows, charred skeleton fingers obtruding, gesturing, beckoning. The glass was a poor protection, but it was all he had: when a sudden gust seemed to open the door a fraction he clung desperately to the glazing bars, tearing his nails in panic.

He must not look, must not acknowledge their presence. Were there words, prayers, intercessions that might help? He tried to remember, but nothing came except images of death, blood, and smashed bone, limbs twitching, eyes glazing – eighteen hours ago?

In spite of himself his head turned slowly, away from the comforting practicality of the code numbers. There, in the glass panes, was his own face, a killing face, and in the light outside surely there were others, black and decayed, the white bone showing through. Surrendering with a single scream he shrank down on the little square floor, arms over his head, trying to retreat into himself, and crying, 'Mary Mother of God save me, Mary Mother of God save me . . .'

As they had promised, the Newcastle men were there within two hours, two of them, a big fellow in a donkey jacket and a smaller man sharply featured and inadequately dressed against such weather. In spite of his insignificant appearance, pale face and narrow shoulders that spoke of generations of under-nourishment and ill-health, he was clearly the leader and a man of decision and authority. Not that Stephen was aware of their coming, for he was still shrunk huddled on the floor, mutter-ing 'Mary, Mother of God –' When the kiosk door opened he began to scream wildly, legs kicking out, arms flailing, striking the glass sides. They hastily shut the door, and looked at each other.

'Christ in heaven, what's got at the man? Is it him, d'you know?' asked the big fellow.

'Aye, its him right enough, Stephen Kiernan,' the small one answered. 'Let's get him into the car out of the way.'

It was not easy. They had to drag him, screaming and tearing at them, into their own car. He was thrown in and the door slammed shut, which seemed to comfort him, for he subsided again, arms over the head, muttering 'Mary, Mother of God.'

'Have you ever seen the like of that before? And what's to be done?' The big man was white himself now: Stephen's nails had slashed his face, and the blood was trickling down.

'It takes them like that sometimes, but I've never seen it as bad, mind. Yesterday was a messy business. You've seen the television.'

'But it wasn't his first time. They told me he was a hard man, and look at him now, will you? He's hardly a man at all.'

The smaller man thought for a moment, opened the door of the car and tried to lay a friendly hand on the killer's shoulder. The screaming started up again immediately, and the door was quickly shut.

'Right, that does it, there's only one thing we can do now. He's a danger to all of us. Switch on the headlamps and pass me that little case.'

Crouched in the lights of the car the small man took some objects from the case and worked neatly and precisely with screwdriver and pliers in the driving rain. When he had finished they got back into their car and drove slowly on up the road, searching for the stranded motor. They found it, just past the gibbet, and pushed and carried their passenger with great difficulty back into the driver's seat. Once again, enclosed and seemingly protected, he was easier, the foul things that were seeking for him shut out; he lay crouched, muttering. The small man removed the petrol filler cap and put something in its place.

'Right now, let's get back, I've only given it five minutes, and I'm soaked.'

Both were tense, imagining the horror of what was happening to the man, and knowing the horror of what would happen. They drove off leaving him to the night and its inhabitants.

Deadwater Gibbet is an isolated spot, as may be seen from the Ordnance Survey map, and especially at that time of year, so it was the following morning before anything amiss was noticed. When the police saw the burnt-out wreck and its contents, not being used to such things they took it hard. The body, charred to a fraction of its former size, had spilled out on to the ground. White bone showed through the blackened flesh and little flakes, like leaves, blew off in the dying wind.

A midsummer entertainment

Canon Robert Gerald Hargreaves was by no means a greedy man, and indeed could be described as one in great measure free from carnal afflictions, but it must be admitted, as he would certainly admit, that he looked forward to his Saturday breakfasts with rather too great a relish.

Clerical stipends are small, and his was all the income Canon and Mrs Hargreaves possessed. To be sure, there were no children to be fed, clothed and educated, which had been an affliction in the past, but now, they both being well into their sixties, was rather cause for relief. And they had that little garden, with some hens, carefully tended by Mrs Hargreaves. Even so, and with inflation as it had been, there was little to spare for breakfasts that went much beyond tea, porridge, toast and home-made marmalade.

Not that he despised these simple meals, especially when they were enlivened by the occasional fresh egg, but still the Canon looked forward to, indeed almost lusted after, his Saturday breakfasts.

Westmorland is good breakfast country, and most of his parishioners would every day enjoy fried eggs, bacon, mushrooms in season, black puddings and a solid length of Cumberland sausage. For one who laboured only in the vineyard of the Lord this would be a surfeit as diurnal nourishment, and when afflicted either by conscience or indigestion the Canon had often thought of giving up his Saturday feast; but his wife prevailed.

A clergyman's weekend, she contended, was a taxing time: when others were at leisure, he had to work at parish meetings, garden parties, visiting, preparing for Sunday – fortunately private confessions were unknown in Westmorland so this was not added to the burden of the wearing business of Sunday services, which must cover the three parishes in his care. A man needed building up for this, and must begin his weekend with a nourishing breakfast. The meal had therefore become not perhaps the highlight of his week, but the event which he most eagerly awaited. To the standard farmer's repast Mrs Hargreaves added freshly ground coffee – a quarter of a pound bought in Penrith every week – and at least one kidney. It was a delight that never palled.

But, especially at the age of sixty-three, a man cannot face such a meal shortly after rising. An interlude of brisk exercise was appropriate and the Canon accordingly took a four-mile walk up to the hilltop and back every Saturday, between 7 and 8.15. This practice was well known to all who lived in the parish, and many of the farmers were in the habit of saving up some bit of news for him as he passed, or even, but rarely, asking in their roundabout way for some advice. On this particular Saturday it was not a farmer, but the schoolmaster, Peter Wainside, who was waiting for him.

Wainside was a man of about thirty who had been brought up in the village, married a girl he met at teacher-training college, and had been successful in being appointed headmaster in the same school where he had been a pupil. He was a cheery, lively and sympathetic man, much liked by both children and parents. At heart he was still much of a child himself, with an impish sense of mischief.

Today this did not appear evident: his customary grin, now become a habitual expression, was belied by worried eyes and looked quite out of place. The Canon, homeward bound at a good pace towards his sausages, was not gratified by the meeting, and Wainside knew better than to detain him long. After the usual exchange of civilities, Wainside said only, 'If you wouldn't mind dropping in at the school after breakfast Canon, I'd be very grateful. There's something I think you ought to see.'

74

The Canon felt a twinge of guilt: gluttony was a terrible sin. He put his breakfast to the hazard. 'If it is urgent, of course I'll come now, Peter.'

'Oh, no, after breakfast will be fine – probably better then. The school, mind you, not the house.'

Had the Canon known what he was to find in the school he would not have enjoyed his excellent breakfast as much as he did. The black pudding, in particular, would have been left on the side of his plate.

As it was, he read the local paper with his coffee – they could not afford to take *The Times* nowadays, at more than £1 a week, so contented themselves with Radio 4 news, but Saturdays were special – tut-tutted over the really quite modest local misdemeanours that, together with market reports, form the staple news of the countryside, finished his toast, beamed at his wife and the world, and set off for the school. He found Wainside in the little domestic-science room that also served as staff kitchen, practical laboratory and home for the school gerbils. There was a peculiar collection of objects spread out on the bench: an old sack, rotten and discoloured, held together only by some black and viscous substance like congealed treacle, half full, the nature of its contents hinted at by a few brown bones that lay beside it.

'Where on earth did you get that disgusting thing?' asked the startled Canon.

Wainside contemplated it with distaste. 'One of the children found it; they often bring in bones – you may remember we found a roe-deer skeleton, and the senior form helped to mount it, a couple of years back? It helps them with their natural history. The kid thought this was something of the same sort.'

'And is it?'

Wainside did not answer but lifted a tea-towel that covered something else lying on the bench.

The Canon rocked back, pale with horror. 'My God, who . . .?' A human skull was looking up from the bench, rather a small skull, mottled yellow and brown, with a few tags of discoloured flesh and patches of red hair still clinging to it.

Wainside quickly replaced the covering. 'It's horrible enough, but I'm afraid the story behind it is even worse. Come into my study and I'll tell you all about it.'

Canon Hargreaves was happy to leave that hideous collection of fragments and to sit down in the small study. Wainside fidgeted for a moment, looking out of the window and wondering how to begin. 'It all started a long time ago, just after you came to the parish. Do you remember that boy Dougie Morrison, from Fellfoot?'

The Canon did. 'Surely that – that – isn't . . .?'

'I am very much afraid it is. Look, I've made some tea. May I tell you the whole story? Perhaps I should have done so a long time ago.'

The Canon signified assent, and Wainside told the story without any interruption other than that incurred by refilling their cups.

'Dougie, you probably recall, was the village "bad boy". He was always the first to start anything, and usually at the centre of any trouble. Even although I was six months older I followed his lead, and got into scrapes with him. He never cared about the consequences of any action, and I've always thought of him as representing a standard of recklessness and irresponsibilty by which any other could be judged. But he had great charm, and I trotted after him. We did all the usual things – tickling trout, shooting pigeons, following the hounds, fell-running, driving tractors, teasing the girls – that growing up boys here do. We had our own territory – from Orton Scar down the valley to the village. It didn't matter who owned the land legally – we were its kings, and went wherever we chose.

'Of course some places were better than others. All those modern clinical milking parlours and slurry pits were pretty dull. We much preferred an old run-down farm like George Cowen's up Oddendale.

'They've gone since, but the family had owned the land for generations, and never made much of a job of it. There isn't

76

enough good land down by the beck to balance the fell grazing. The whole thing is too high to be viable nowadays, and George had just about given up. He only made a pretence of farming, kept a couple of cows and some pigs, and lived off the grazing rents. All he had to do was to keep the fences up, and he didn't do that very well, just plugging the gaps with anything that lay to hand – hurdles, old bedsteads, chicken wire. And everything, of course, tied up with binder twine. It was what they call a "right scrow".'

'As a result it was a paradise for us. Crows, rabbits and foxes had a wonderful time around all the neglected dykes and putrefying carcasses – he would never bury any of the fallen stock. We could have a go at the vermin any time we wanted, and use his buildings without any fear of interference. He was too lazy to chase us off, and we got on rather well with him. We were, all of us, pretty much disapproved of by upright hardworking neighbours and elders.

'It would have been the summer of '52 that we went to give him a hand with his hay crop. He had only the one field, and poor stuff at that, with no proper equipment. None of his neighbours would help him since he never thought of doing anything for them. He really was a surly and difficult character.

'He was like that when we turned up. He'd managed to get the grass cut but not properly turned. It was doing itself no good, and unless a few hours' work was put in it would likely be ruined. When we found him, up in the house, he showed no sign of doing anything, told us to push off, that he'd better things to do than fret about the hay. Rather oddly there were some indications that he had made attempts to tidy himself up. He was wearing boots, not clogs, and had shaved – both unusual on a week-day; and we suspected something was afoot. Anything that was better than hay must be interesting, we reckoned, so we hung around in the cover of a stone dyke and watched.

'After a little while Cowen must have roused himself to action and started to make the first of several journeys to a field house in the garth some distance away from the farmhouse. His field houses, which were really just feed stores but substantially built of stone and slate, like those dotted around all fellside farms, had survived more or less intact without any attention from him. From the things he was carrying – planks and trestles, lanterns and other oddments – it looked as though he intended to make the field house temporarily habitable. But who might want to use one of Cowen's field houses, which must be in a state of filth and disorder, was a mystery. We couldn't imagine any locals, even if they'd happened to want somewhere for a camp meeting or shepherds' meet, choosing such a remote and unpleasant location. Something out of the ordinary must be up, so we decided to hang around behind the dyke and see if anybody came up the track from the village.

'We didn't have long to wait for Cowen's visitors. They came in a coach, edging gingerly up the narrow lane, having to stop at every gate to open and shut it, driven by a man nervous for his paintwork. Apart from him the bus was full of women of all ages and sizes, large ladies in hats and flowered dresses, younger ones with short hair and slacks. It might have been a Mother's Union outing, or a temperance rally, or the Rose Society.

'Once our curiosity had been aroused it had to be satisfied. We waited for the coach to unload its passengers at the farm and make its way back. As it stopped at the first gate on its return journey we accosted the driver and offered to open the gates for him. Since otherwise he would have had to climb down at every gate, open it – an operation rendered tricky by Cowen's reliance on binder twine – climb back, drive forward and dismount once more to close it, he accepted our invitation. While Dougie did the gates, I, being the intellectual one whose job it was to find out what was up, talked to the man. He was ready enough with his information, for what it was worth. It seemed that the ladies were members of some historical society or other from the West Riding, who came to places of interest for some sort of meeting. He didn't know what they did; perhaps they sketched and took photographs. They stayed the night and he collected them the next day. This was the second year they had come to Cowen's farm, on the exact same date, too.

'Now we knew even then that historians did frequent odd and uncomfortable places, and we had plenty of such around for them to choose from. The fell is full of the remains of Celtic villages, standing stones and dolmens, as you well know. We had heard that Uther Pendragon was supposed to have held his court at Lyvennet, and had met the Arthurians who came questing for its location; but Cowen's farm? It was a good mile from the nearest ruin we knew of, and we had never heard of any interest attaching to it.

'There was plenty more for us to think about, however, and by the next day we had forgotten all about the goings on at Cowen's farm. We were kept pretty busy through the summer and autumn with school holidays, village shows, sheepdog trials, beating for the shoots, and it must have been near midwinter before we crossed Cowen's land again.

'We had been out with the Ullswater hounds up on Asby Fell and were taking a short cut home when we smelled something odd and unpleasant in the cold air. The stench of decomposing sheep was not uncommon on Odden Farm, but this seemed to come from somewhere up in a clump of trees, and was odd enough to tempt us to take a look. We cast around a bit, and traced the smell to a sack hung on a battered old oak covered in mistletoe. It was high, out of reach even if we had wanted to investigate further, but when Dougie threw a stone at it the stench grew much worse, and the brown liquid that dropped from it – there were maggots in it – discouraged us from closer examination. Tea called, and we were off.

'I did wonder whether there might be any connection with what had been going on in the field house, and took a look round it soon after. It was like the dog that didn't bark in the night: there was nothing there, and that was remarkable. Usually I would have expected a terrible muddle of old straw, sacks of concrete gone solid, unused fertilizer, rusting implements, empty cans, bits of wood, chicken wire and all the detritus of the lazy farmer. But everything was tolerably clean, if not exactly swept and garnished; it must have been the tidiest spot on the whole farm.

'Ater that it was a good six months before we thought about it again. In that short time – things happen quickly at that age – Dougie and I had grown somewhat apart. I had started studying, while Dougie was being more helpful about the farm. We were both also getting rather more interested in girls than in hanging about with the lads. Nevertheless, when Dougie came to tell me that he had seen the same busload of women making for Cowen's farm, I did not need much persuading to go off with him to see what they really got up to.

'We waited until after dark. It wasn't too difficult to get away, for boys always slip out at nights for a bit of poaching, but we had to wait until late before it was near dark enough. I didn't realize it at the time, but it was Midsummer Eve.

'There was a strange atmosphere about this expedition, something quite different from the usual night spent ticing pheasants. We didn't know what to expect but felt somehow drawn, quite inevitably, up Oddendale to Cowen's farm. Sure enough, a light was shining from the field house. We approached it cautiously enough: we were pretty good at moving silently. You know that field houses don't have windows, just narrow slits for ventilation. We each found a convenient slit and looked in.

'Cowen, who was nowhere to be seen, must have provided a number of Tilley lamps, those paraffin pressure-lamps, each of which created a bright circle of light, although it was dark enough in the shadows between them. Everything was confused, but what we could see took our breath away: the space was full of figures moving together as if they were in some sort of dance.

'The really exciting thing – remember we were boys of thirteen – was that all the dancing figures were female, and all were naked. We'd never really seen a woman without clothes on, just bits of somebody's sister and such like, and these were all ages, shapes and sizes – long-legged girls with little bumps of breasts to floppy grandmothers, all enthrallingly curved and shadowed.

'When we had recovered our wits we could make out, although with some difficulty, what was happening. The women were moving round a flat stone on which something lay. At regular intervals during the dance (if that was what it was) one woman after another would go up to the slab and throw herself on top of it, and on top of whatever was on it. As one girl – she was a real beauty – did so, a gap in the circle appeared that let us see more clearly.

'The thing on the slab was the body – bloody, white and hairy – of a sheep or a calf, slit down the belly. After each woman had mounted it, she rose all bloodied and went back to embrace the others. All this was done rhythmically to the accompaniment of something like a flute, and to chanting which rose to a crescendo every time a woman went to the slab.

'It wasn't at all wild or manic: that was one of the horrible things about it. The women seemed very serious, sedate, disciplined, almost like the parody of a church social, in fact. I couldn't understand the chant, but a shudder seemed to run through the – congregation, I thought of it as – when one of them embraced the others. Apart from that they showed no emotion. I suppose they might have been drugged.

'Dougie was enthralled, and whispered to me that he was going to try for a better view. I stayed where I was, fascinated and terrified at the same time. Dougie could do what he wanted; I wasn't going to miss a minute, yet in a funny sort of way I didn't want to see anything more clearly.

'Then, suddenly, the whole scene changed. There was a scuffling noise at the door – Dougie, I suppose – and a flurry of movement and outburst of noise. The women stopped dancing and dashed for the door, shrieking, furious, fingers crooked, arms outstretched, hair flowing, breasts bouncing, real maenads.

81

'I didn't stop to find out what happened but ran home as fast as I could, scrambling over gates and dykes. I reached my bed shivering and weeping.

'Needless to say, Dougie was missing next morning. Nobody was too much fussed to begin with, but after twenty-four hours they began to get worried, and the police were called in. You probably remember the rest. No trace of Dougie was ever found, but the fells are so wild that a small body could lie there undisturbed for centuries – not to mention the potholes and old lead-workings.

'I kept absolutely quiet. It wouldn't have done any good if I had told them, and I couldn't even bring myself to think of what might have happened to Dougie. After a few months I went back to the field house, but there was no sign of anything. The farm grew even more neglected, and Cowen sold up for what he could get and left the district.

'Then, just yesterday, young Jamie Thomson found that sack. It must have rotted through and dropped off the tree: it was in the same copse where we'd seen one like it. Thank God he didn't look inside. I suppose the calf, or whatever, was hung up in a tree after the ceremony. They must have killed Dougie and shoved his body in the same sack – a sort of double sacrifice.'

The poor Canon was horrified. It was not so much that he was ignorant of the darker manifestations of human behaviour as that he kept them categorized: wanton violence was to be expected in cities, or in wartime, but not here in the peaceful Westmorland countryside. People had their dark secrets here, as everywhere, but not this . . . Yet he was aware of the old religion, witchcraft, and its survivals; he knew the significance of oak trees, mistletoe, the Beltane fires of midsummer; and he recalled that on the fell above Cowen's farm were more than twenty ancient sacrificial sites and standing stones. Oddendale took its name from the god Odin, the supreme god of the Vikings, and had in those times been a centre for all kinds of pagan rites including the worship of the cannibal goddess

Eostre, who gave her name to the Christian Easter. But these surely were matters for guides and history books, not the stuff of daily life? People didn't do things like that. Even as he formulated the thought he knew it to be wrong: they did, oh yes, they did. He took a long breath.

'Are you quite sure, Peter, that those, those remains, are those of your friend?'

'I'm afraid there's no doubt. Dougie had that unmistakable red hair, and besides – although I haven't looked at all closely, you'll understand – I saw one of those little belt clasps in the form of a snake. Dougie wore one. But what am I going to do? Have I got to go to the police?'

The Canon had all the reflexes of the middle-class Englishman; his instinct in any trouble was to appeal to the police. But now he wasn't too sure. The case was long since closed, and it would be impossible to track down the women after such a lapse of time, not to speak of identifying the actual killers. If the discovery of these wretched remains was to be disclosed, Dougie's family, who had by now come to terms with his disappearance, would have all that pain to go through again, as well as the added unhappiness of knowing that his decomposing body had been hanging there, a mile from his home, unburied. And perhaps even worse, hundreds of prurient sightseers, avid for ghoulish thrills, would descend on his village and disturb the tranquil lives of his parishioners.

Looking at Peter, who, in spite of his outwardly calm appearance, was clearly holding on to his emotions very tightly, Canon Hargreaves knew where his duty lay. 'No, Peter, I don't think that would serve any useful purpose. You have done what you should have done by telling me this awful story, and I will see that the remains of this poor boy are properly taken care of. Now please go; tell my wife I shall be detained for some time, and leave me to do what is necessary.'

The schoolmaster was infinitely relieved by this, and although he stammered a few guilty thanks he took his leave with a light heart. The Canon went reluctantly back into the kitchen-laboratory to start his disagreeable task. He found a pair of rubber gloves and some plastic sacks: he did what he could with the horrid mess in the sack but, being no anatomist, could not be entirely sure which bones were calf and which boy. Making some fairly arbitrary decisions he divided the remains among two of the sacks. Disposing of the one containing what he hoped was the calf, he thought with some grim satisfaction, would be Peter Wainside's job. The boot of Wainside's car and a convenient hole up on the fell would suffice for that.

The rest was his own responsibility and must find a resting-place in consecrated ground. He could hardly dig a suitable grave unobserved, so he placed the bones as reverently as possible in a small vault inside the church, which had belonged to a family long since defunct. They would be safe there for many years yet.

In later days, examining his conscience over the matter, he was glad that he had done this himself rather than choosing some more public course of action, not only for the reasons that had first led him to do so, but following something he discovered while he was attempting to sort out the bones.

Dougie's hands and feet had been tied together, a fact which presented the horrifying possibility, to put it no higher, that he had been alive when stuffed in the sack. The boy might have lived for days in the dark, with the carcase of the calf, the putrefaction, the maggots, the stench and the terror. And he might have been saved if his friend had possessed the courage to tell his story in time.

The Canon did not think that the schoolmaster could well have lived with this realization. He himself found it very disturbing; he looked at the meetings of the Women's Institute with a newly suspicious eye, and entirely eschewed black puddings for the rest of his life.

The Jews' Tower

The English were, beyond doubt, a nation of filthy, tea-drinking sluts, devoid of any concept of decency or order. Dr Pablo Aguila surveyed the boardroom of Brancepeth-Helmsley Industries, where he had been left sitting, with some disgust. The great mahogany table was littered with papers, dirty tea-cups, biscuit crumbs and ash-trays. 'Forgive us, Dr Aguila,' the chairman had said, 'if we leave you for a few minutes while we discuss your proposed amendments. Please make yourself at home.' As though any home of his would be in so disgusting a mess!

The chairman was typically English, too. Tall, very tall, thin, pale-blue eyes and too much fair hair. Aguila was familiar with the type. He had seen them before, nothing soldierly about them, wearing silk scarves, pullovers and suede boots – suede boots, God help us! – and so damned calm and condescending: amiable enough, in their smug way, but no order, no discipline.

Look at this room, the boardroom of a distinguished old company. The walls, dusted only as far as the cleaner could reach, covered with whiskery portraits of past directors, medals mounted in glass cases, won at international exhibitions of the last century and a large painting of some seaplane they had built in the First World War. Nothing was more recent than 1917! The furniture was massively Victorian; a few of the chairs had little silver plaques recording some visit when a royal behind had rested upon them. When would these people be dragged into the twentieth century?

But now they were coming back into the room, not in any order of seniority as any group of his race would have sorted

85

themselves, but in some inconsequential muddle. All had, it seemed, been agreed; but even so there was no formal document yet produced. Only a handshake, one of those stupid 'gentleman's agreements'. The memorandum of terms would follow, with the contract coming even later. He would never accept it from the North Americans, but the English – and damn them for it – could be trusted.

There were handshakes all round, and expressions of mutual esteem. The chairman was to drive his guest back to the hotel himself, a courtesy which both men could well have done without. Aguila looked with obvious distaste at the low, elegant car: it was the sort of thing for a film actor, not a respectable businessman. For his part, Martin Helmsley, chairman and controlling shareholder of Brancepeth-Helmsley Industries, was a man who embraced obligations in proportion as he found them distasteful. He could be seen, always in the same suit of rather shabby tweeds, with the same air of abstract courtesy, bending over to listen to auditors, shop stewards, parish ladies, reporters, or any of the other troublesome folk who make a chairman's life difficult. In general he did this willingly enough, for he found humanity usually likeable, if less so than either horses or dogs; but he did not like Aguila in the least. As a result he was almost painfully cordial, to the point of effusiveness.

While the discussions had been progressing – he had taken no very active part in them, leaving the financial and marketing directors to do the bulk of the work – Helmsley had been studying Aguila. The man was of an age to have taken part in the last war, but didn't have the air of a soldier, even allowing for the passing of the years. There was a humorless fussiness about him which most men who have seen service get beaten out of them.

Nor did he volunteer any information about his past, his wife or family, politics, sport or anything not entirely relevant to the business in hand. Luncheon had been a difficult meal, as topic after topic was discarded in the attempt to make polite conversation.

They had now a fifty-minute drive in front of them, so the problem presented itself anew. Aguila made manifest his disapproval of the car, making much of the difficulty of fitting into the passenger seat, which indeed was not the easiest thing for a man of his habit of body, and of stowing his possessions in the cramped rear seats. It is true that the Jensen Interceptor is not the most capacious of cars, and that a more conventional chairman might have chosen differently, but Helmsley felt confirmed in his impression that Aguila, although tough enough in business matters, was something of an old woman rather than an old soldier.

As a result he drove more slowly than usual, punishing himself for a breach of good manners, and cast about for a topic of conversation that might last out the journey. This emerged soon enough, as it transpired that Aguila, rather than returning that afternoon to London, proposed to spend the rest of the day in York visiting the Minster and the other sights of that splendid old city. Helmsley felt an almost proprietorial interest in his county's capital, and launched enthusiastically into a well practised speech.

'We're very proud of our history in York. We've certainly got the best-preserved medieval city in England. Of course on the Continent, where the Industrial Revolution came later and people had the sense to preserve their past, you have many more – Cordoba, for instance –' this as a gesture to Aguila's present nationality, 'Prague, and . . .' Helmsley was about to say Nuremberg, but felt that a discordant note might thereby be struck '. . . and besides, after the Tudors settled things there was no need to keep up town walls except round some coastal cities – Berwick has some very fine Elizabethan walls, and what is left at Southampton after that barbaric Council has had its way is still impressive. But York has by far the finest range of medieval walls. Look, you can see them now.'

The city was just coming into view, with a continuous battlemented wall in strikingly white limestone on a fresh green bank, useless as a defensive work since the invention of cannon, but looking decorative and romantic in the early summer sunshine. Behind it the grey stones and red-tiled roofs rose to the crest of the hill and the massive towers of the Minster. Aguila acknowledged it to be an impressive sight.

'We have to make a half-circuit of the walls to reach the hotel. That large building behind the wall there is one of the guild-halls, Merchant Taylors'. Just like London, York had all the medieval guilds, its own mint, and hall-marks. It was the second town of the realm – they've got a sword in the Guildhall that was given to the Mayor by the Emperor Sigismund, the one that had Hus burned. And on this side of the walls is Jewbury, the old Jewish cemetery. Jews had to be interred outside the walls, of course. We once had the largest Jewish community outside London.'

Aguila felt annoyed by the reference. Jews played no part in the great history of the Aryan races, and the English were certainly Aryan. Besides, the mention of Jews, especially dead ones, always made him uncomfortable: the juxtaposition of the idea of burning was also unfortunate. Helmsley, sensing this, pursued the subject with a naughty relish. 'Now we turn right into Castlegate. Up there is the castle mound, and the ruin on top was the old keep. It used to be called Clifford's Tower, but it's often known as the Jews' Tower, especially since 1190.'

Aguila felt forced to say something, but managed no more than, 'Oh, yes.'

Helmsley was able to construe the remark as a question. 'It was an unsettling period. There was a deal of anti-Jewish hysteria at the time – little St Hugh of Lincoln, Christian babies being killed for Jewish sacrifices – it was all nonsense, but ruffians took advantage of it – there are some of them about in every age, you know – and incited the York mob to a pitch of excitement where they rounded up all the Jews they could find, women and children included, herded them into that tower, and quite literally roasted them alive. Built fires all around the tower till the walls became red-hot. Took some little time.

Anyway, it discouraged the others and there were no more Jews in York after that.

'In a funny way it marked the end of the city's prosperity. There were other reasons – the Ouse silted up, and the rise in the coal industry, which really took off in the sixteenth century, transferred the commercial primacy to Newcastle – *they* kept the hall-mark, for instance, so that our silversmiths had to go there to have their work assayed. The commercial greatness of York was gone.

'Our Anglo-Saxon and Norman forebears, like all their fellow-Teutons, come to that' – here he glanced at Aguila, but found an expressionless face – 'thought the highest duty of man lay in knocking others about. They didn't care much for the arts, or for trade. The great cathedrals, the statues, and everything else we revere them for, were the work of artisans. The gentry wouldn't soil their hands with anything except blood, so the Jews very obligingly took over the business of finance, and did it very well.

'Things haven't changed all that much, either. All the London banks were founded by Jews, Germans, Scotchmen or Welshmen – just look at the names. Rothschild, Baring, Barclay, Lloyd, Schroder, Lazard, Williams – not an English name among them. Even today the real English are still farmers, fighters, travellers or poets at heart, and not much good for anything else.'

By this time Aguila was angry and uncomfortable. It was obvious that the Englishman was using this story of the Jews to attack him, and that he suspected something. Aguila was not going to give him the satisfaction of exhibiting any response. When they reached the hotel he extricated himself from the car with as much dignity as possible. 'Thank you, Mr Chairman, for your most interesting description, and the trouble you have given yourself driving me here. I shall much look forward to visiting your great city, which I will now proceed to do, and trust to the speedy conclusion of our business together.'

Helmsley was slightly disappointed as he drove off; he was

sure that the man had been a Nazi, and although that would not have stopped him from doing business with him – there had been so many of them, after all – he had wanted to make the fellow squirm a bit.

He had succeeded better than he knew. Aguila stood in front of the hall-porter's desk for a moment, much inclined to ask the man the time of the next train for London, before pulling himself together, sticking to his plans, and asking the porter instead for a good guide-book. Arming himself with this, he spent half an hour drinking coffee and planning a route which would take in all those sights the guide specially recommended, before setting off briskly. He had chosen a route that took him first over the Ouse and past the Museum gardens and Multangular Roman tower to the Minster, before walking on through the town, visiting the famous Shambles, to the castle and thence back to the hotel.

This programme he followed with great thoroughness, not dawdling but conscientiously examining everything the guide-book had told him to admire. He was nearly finished with the Minster, having reached the famous grisaille window known as the Five Sisters, when the setting sun, finding the exact angle, exploded through the window in a shower of grey-green light. Heavens, it must be late! There was only just enough time to walk back through the Shambles to the hotel, if he was to be there in time to bath before dinner.

He would certainly not be able to visit the castle with its tower. Regrettable, of course, but it could not be helped: it was simply that there was not enough time; there was no question, of course, of his evading the visit.

The walk back to the hotel was therefore brisk: the Shambles admired – so like Bamberg – but at a smart pace. He was able, without undue haste but with small opportunity for loitering, to bath (carefully folding up his dirty linen and placing it in the bag reserved for that purpose), to clean his teeth with the correct number of strokes, to dress in the garments proper for dinner in a large hotel, and leave everything in its correct place. It was so important, especially when travelling, to observe high standards of order. He presented himself promptly at the dining-room.

The Royal Station Hotel at York is perhaps only in the second rank of hotels, but the view from its dining-room can hardly be surpassed. With his smoked salmon and glass of Bernkastler he saw the loom of the Minster gradually thicken and blend into the dark sky. Then, suddenly and unexpectedly – *augenblicklich*! – the floodlights were switched on and the great cathedral was incandescent with light and dramatic with shadows.

It was so magnificent a spectacle that only with difficulty did he manage to pay his sweetbreads the attention they deserved; but when they, and the Stilton and the last of the bottle of Vosne Romanée were despatched he was able to savour the sight without distraction. It was truly impressive, a masterpiece of Gothic civilization.

The food and drink had brought a new confidence to Aguila. It was a fine night, and a stroll would be welcome; indeed he might repair the omission of that afternoon and pay a visit to the castle. Accordingly, after choosing a good Havana, he sallied forth, prudently putting on a light overcoat against the chill of even a summer evening in Yorkshire.

The night was fragrant, both with the stocks planted round the city walls and his cigar, and having reached the castle he took his place on a convenient bench to admire the ruined tower, floodlit like the Minster.

It was stupid to think, after all these years, about those Jews. After all, Dachau had not been an extermination camp: those were the really bad places. No Jews had been killed in Dachau, apart of course from the entirely proper execution of trouble-makers. There had, it was true, been many deaths, some of them perhaps from the experiments, but the Jews were a feeble race and had not been able to stand the inevitable hardships of camp life. He had nothing to reproach himself with. Even those righteous Englishmen had gone in for roasting Jews.

He admired the tower again. So that was where the English had burnt *their* Jews! He might as well examine it more closely.

With some difficulty he climbed the fence and scrambled up the mound, pausing, somewhat out of breath, in the shadows just before the floodlights. He became aware, as he stood, of an insistent buzzing, pulsating, irregular, noise somewhere near: perhaps an electrical fault? He was moved by some whim to draw closer to the tower and passed the floodlights to reach the wall itself.

As he did so the light caught him and threw his shadow, grotesquely deformed and enlarged, on the wall – a *kobold*, gnome or forest monster. The humming increased, and became a torrent of sound, wailing, shrieking, bellowing, groaning, cursing, combining into an overwhelming cry of terror and pain. He could smell that smell, too, the one he had forgotten about for forty years; unmistakable, penetrating, acrid. He stumbled, falling against the wall of the tower, tearing his fingers on the stone.

All his senses were assailed at once. He felt the cold stone of the castle freeze under a blast of ice that set him shivering; smelt the terrible odour of burning carcasses that starts as an almost appetizing smell of roasting meat but changes as the flesh is consumed and the bones begin to char; and, worst of all, heard the chorus of shrill agitated cries. He had a glimpse of a boyhood holiday on the Baltic coast when a dead whale had been washed ashore: the seagulls had made just such a noise, voracious, their beaks open, waiting their turn to tear a strip from the decaying flesh.

But these noises were worse, agonized, having a semblance of humanity in their cries which seemed like words: the raucous shrieks became "*Rache, rache . . .*" the cries that dying Jews might make, calling for vengeance on their tormentors.

The tower, with its memories of cruelty and death, must be the centre of this! He tried to escape, to run down the mound, but felt himself pinned between the light and the tower, his powers dissolving. With a huge effort of will he made a dash, stumbled, fell, and rolled down the slope, tearing at the turf for a hold, to the ditch at the bottom. Ahead of him was a bank surmounted by a wire-mesh fence, with the lights of the road beyond. An image of another fence, with watchtowers and searchlights, came to him, and he felt that if only he could get to the other side of the fence, away from the malevolent cries and the fearful smell, he might be safe.

Somehow, covered in sweat, his heart pounding he scrambled up the bank and flung himself on the fence, hauling himself up, scrabbling at the links. His clothes were torn by the barbed wire but he didn't care. He dropped down on the other side. The worst of the shrieking had died down but had left him with a terrible pain across his head; it felt as though his skull was crushing the brain inside. The street lights seemed to flare and diminish; images of the buildings moved into and out of focus. His lungs seemed full of solid matter, but he managed to drag himself on to a bench where he collapsed.

The three youths had had an unsatisfactory evening. Two pubs had refused to serve them on account of their bizarre appearance. Kev and Mart were in their leathers, big boys both of them, massively studded and mauve-haired, but relatively harmless. Scut, although weedy, was the dangerous one; he wore a jacket, its sleeves rolled up to uncover studded wristbands, red-and-black striped trousers held up by a studded belt, a T-shirt with an Iron Cross, and a swastika pendant. He stood back during the fights, but did the damage when the others got their victim on the ground. They had eventually found a crowded bar where they were served by a barmaid too nervous to refuse, and picked a squabble with a couple of crop-haired squaddies. Things were just beginning to look interesting when the landlord turned up. He was a solid sixteen stones of flesh, with an aggressive air and each hand grasping a beer bottle. They were out in the street, their drinks unfinished, before they could manage more than a couple of curses.

Following this humiliation they were in a thoroughly nasty mood as they walked back to their van. The old drunk lying on the bench, grunting and retching, seemed to promise some amusement. They gave him a kick to stir him up a bit.

Aguila welcomed the pain lancing into his consciousness: that way forgiveness might lie, a refuge from the furies that were tormenting him. He did not try to avoid that kick, or the ones that followed, but turned to welcome them. As he did so he saw Scut, the Iron Cross and the swastika dangling in front of him. He might have known! The boys would not forget him. They would fetch him clear of those damned Jews: that had just been a moment of weakness, then. '*Komm hier, Kamerad, ich bin hart bedrängt.*'

He stretched out his arms towards Scut, who saw only a dirty old man trying to paw him, and recoiled in disgust. 'Fucking old bastard, I'll fix him.'

Before the others could stop him, if indeed they tried to do, Scut pulled a plastic bottle from his jacket pocket and flung its contents over the grovelling old man. Striking a match, he threw it and jumped back at the same time, hustling the horrified Kev and Mart away from the screaming, blazing, thing writhing on the bench.

The Buff and the Blue

The Reverend Harold Dickson Ridley opened the last box and started putting the final books on the shelves. They included Bishop Creighton's *History of the Papacy*, a favourite for bedside reading, and the many volumes of the Century Bible and Cruden's *Concordance*, the essential tools of his trade. He was by now skilled in unpacking, for Methodist ministers are transferred to new churches every few years and this was to be the final post of his ministry.

He had almost come full circle since his ordination nearly forty years before: for the first time since he started college, apart from a few short visits, he was back in his native county of Durham, to serve in a pit village not unlike that in which he had been born and bred.

The circuit steward who had been helping him picked up the empty box.

'Why noo, Mistor Ridley, that's the last of the byuks. It's always a problem to find enough room in the Manse for byuks, but we've done wor best for you with the shelves, though wood's hard to come by. Willie Wilkinson, the pit joiner, made them with some offcuts. What they lack in elegance they've got in strength, like some of us, perhaps.'

The Manse Committee had done its best to make the big Victorian house comfortable, although post-war shortages made life difficult. At any rate the Ridleys would never be short of coal: the committee members, almost all pit men, would see to that.

Mrs Ridley, who had been wiping the books with a waxed cloth as her husband put them on the shelves, answered him.

'I'm sure we'll be very happy among you, Mr Walker. We've seen a lot of places, but there's nobody as kind and friendly as Durham folk, as I know well.'

'So they tell us; it's a difficult life enough, and we do what we can to make it easier. And talking of that, my missus has made a bite of tea, I know. It's time we all had a bit rest.'

As well as cleaning the Manse to that degree of sparkling perfection that miners' wives consider normal, Mrs Walker had provided a formidable tea. 'Nothing bought here – bread, cakes, and jam home-made, ham home-cooked. One thing the rationing's done, it's taught the young 'uns that they're better off making their own, I say.'

Later that evening, when the Ridleys had been settled in to general satisfaction, Harold was able to take a look at his new surroundings. Leaving his wife in front of a well-banked fire, he climbed out of the village up the hillside to a spot which gave him both a view and a convenient seat on a fallen log, and surveyed the scene with some contentment.

It was a landscape redolent of coal. Every chimney poured out fumes, giving the air a pungent carboniferous quality: the great rounded slag-heaps formed the eastern horizon, and below them the lights of the colliery sparkled as the night shift surface-workers got on with grading and washing. There was something compelling and unnatural about a pit: the great effort of tearing out vast quantities from the earth's interior and piling them on the surface, leaving huge voids beneath the soil, seemed a savage reversal of God's order. Like a gaping wound showing the underside of the skin, or more prosaically, a jacket turned inside out, the landscape showed things as their creator – God or tailor – had not meant them to be.

Well, there was a price to be paid for it all.

He remembered his first time underground, sixty years ago. He had been just seven years old at the time; it was, of course, strictly forbidden for children, but his father had taken him, and James Ridley was a difficult man to resist. Just over thirty, he was already a fore-overman at Usworth Main, and doing well enough with his certificates to expect an under-manager's post before too long. A good-humoured man, he could usually joke and jolly his shift into co-operation and make light of the always uncomfortable and often dangerous conditions below ground. Usworth was an old pit with narrowing seams and little clearance, where hard work and skill was needed to make a decent living. If there was trouble – and this was invariably on the surface rather than underground, for men working on the face have no surplus energy for violent disagreements – James could be relied upon to settle it, almost always peaceably.

A recalcitrant workman had to be very foolish to proceed to violent measures with James Ridley, who was tall for a miner, only a couple of inches off six feet, and the most powerful man in the pit. He could lift a tub back on to the rails with one hand, as he had once had to do while dragging an injured man clear, or effortlessly straighten the blacksmith's tools. Only once had he hit a man, and the resulting injuries – the unfortunate fellow was hurled backwards over a bench, and was out of work for several weeks – were so shocking that James swore never to strike a man again; and had never, as his reputation became well known, needed to do so.

So when James felt that it was time that young Harry, his eldest son, saw the coalface, the putter-on looked elsewhere and the men were ready to welcome the lad. Harry never thereafter forgot his first trip underground: the terrifying speed of the descent in the cage, 200 fathoms down to the seam; the thud of the compressor and the hiss of the air driving the Winstanley cutters, the ride in the tub to the face, in blackness total except for the subdued glow of the Davy lamps; the friendliness of the men, who seemed only white circles of eyes in the gloom; and above all the smell. A mixture of coal-dust, damp, powder-fumes, lamp oil, horses and human sweat, the odour of the mine was to remain with Harry to his dying day, bringing to mind the comradeship and affection of the men who six days a week toiled together, trusting each other, at their hard and dangerous work, in a companionship which made a perilous and un-

97

friendly world bearable. And it was his own father whom all these wonderful men acknowledged as their leader.

On his return home, glamorously dirty, he was allowed the first bath in front of the kitchen fire and felt that he had achieved the height of human felicity. He was enthralled by it all, and there and then had decided that, come what may, he would go down the mine with his father as soon as he was able. That, after the legislation of 1882, would not be until he was fourteen. It seemed a long time to wait, and most unfair since his father and others of this generation had been earning money underground as putters at the age of ten.

His mother had, however, different views, and although James Ridley might be undisputed ruler on his shift, he deferred on all other matters to his wife. Eliza Ridley had been a teacher before she married, and it was her encouragement and coaching that had forced her husband, who in spite of his many qualities was not immune to the temptations of idleness – temptations which a fifty-four-hour week would make irresistible to most men – through his certificates.

Eliza was determined that her first-born would not go down the pit. It was to be the ministry for him, which inevitably meant, in a Durham pit village, the Methodist ministry, Wesleyan or Primitive. Eliza was Wesleyan, the more sedate of the connections, and her family followed. Two services on Sunday for the grown-ups, Sunday school for the children, class meetings every month, sisterhood meetings once a fortnight, the whole social life of the Ridleys centred on the chapel. Even family gatherings – weddings, birthdays, christenings, funerals – ended up in the front parlour with Eliza playing hymn tunes on the harmonium and everyone joining in with gusto. There were lay tunes too: 'The Waters of Tyne', 'The Keel Row', 'The Hexhamshire Lass', and all the other fine Northumbrian songs. James was particularly fond of 'The Hexhamshire Lass', a jaunty moss-trooping song.

Hey for the buff and the blue,
Hey for cap and the feather,
Hey for the bonnie lass
That lives in Hexhamshire.

He hummed and whistled it whenever life seemed good.

Surprisingly, perhaps, to modern eyes, life often seemed good. With Eliza's intelligent management, and James' wage as deputy, the family was always warm and well fed. If they were never idle for a moment they were equally never bored. Newcastle and Sunderland were only a few miles away, and while music halls were, of course, unthinkable, there were concerts, oratorios – *Elijah* and *Messiah* in season and Shakespeare.

James was also an excellent story-teller. When he was working night shifts, and was about the house and lively when the children came home from school, he would tell them stories of the mine. It was best on winter evenings after tea, around the fire in the kitchen banked high with coal; the stories were usually frightening, and the firelight, with the gas turned down, enhanced the effect.

Some were believable enough: the terrible explosions of fire-damp that had torn men apart and the falls of rock that trapped them. James had once opened up a section of the pit that had been blocked off by a fall nearly a hundred years before. He had found the bodies of the men and ponies just as they had died of thirst and starvation – lying or sitting, the ponies still tied in their stalls, preserved in the dead atmosphere only to crumble when the air came in.

Other stories were more difficult to credit: of the ghosts of men who had died below ground in past centuries (for these mines had been worked since Roman times), and of the goblins for whom placatory saucers of milk were left out to ensure that they bore the miners no ill will.

It was, however, the chapel that was the heart and centre of their social life. Young Harry found there something of the warmth and friendliness that he had experienced during his

99

visit to the pit. The same men, scrubbed pink and shining in respectable black suits, grinned at him and rumpled his hair. The smell was different – carbolic soap, polish, and moth-balls – but carried the same message of a united community. He was, if he had been super-eminently virtuous, allowed to pump the organ, which required both vigour and a feel for the music, and at such times he felt almost reconciled to the idea of minister's life. Most of the preachers were laymen, often miners themselves: a visiting ordained minister was greeted with some deference and offered a sumptuous tea on the best china.

But Harry remained faithful to his vision of life down the pit, picturing himself swinging along with his deputy's lamp and stick, in big pit boots, the object of universal admiration.

Those dreams came to a sudden stop in his eleventh year. He had not been more than an hour at school one morning when he was summoned to the headmaster's study. Old Geordie Lumley, normally aloof and imperturbable, was shocked and distressed. 'Harry, lad, you're to go straight home to your mother. There's been an accident at the pit, and you'd best all be together. There's no news yet, but it was on your father's shift.'

Harry remembered the terrible day, waiting. Eliza was not going to rush to the pit, getting in the way: she would bide at home, and look after her children, and pray. It was five before the manager dashed up to the house in his dogcart, in his working clothes, and filthy. His mother and the manager were alone in the parlour for quarter of an hour before the manager came out.

'You must be a brave boy, Harry. You're the man of the family now. Look after your mother.'

Eliza, a strong-minded woman, needed no assistance. The possibility of sudden death lived always with a miner's family, and she was in control of herself from the first moment. Even so, she could not bring herself to speak of the accident, and it was from the manager next day, when he called to see what help was needed that Harry learned the details.

'There were some men, Harry, working on the face, in a

different part of the mine. They were overcome by choke damp – but one managed to stagger back to the shaft. Your father got a rescue team together straight away, and went to get the men out. They had aerophores with them, and got there all right, but just as they were bringing these men out there was a fall in the gob goaf. It was a big one, and blocked their way out. Normally it wouldn't have mattered, but there was the gas. It was a race against time, then, Harry. We had to get to them before it did. And we nearly managed it, but we were too late for your father. There wasn't enough oxygen, and he gave his to the others: he was by far the strongest and he might have lasted out, but some of the men were close to panic, and so he cheered them up by joking and singing hymns. We could hear him, as we got nearer, "*Guide me, O thou Great Redeemer, Pilgrim thro' this barren land*," he was singing. He kept them alive, breathing steadily, but couldn't do the same for himself. He died just before we got to them. The others will be all right, and they know they owe it all to your father.'

The tragedy had effects tending in opposite directions: the drama of his father's heroic end made Harry more determined to follow in his footsteps; but Eliza for her part was equally adamant that he should not go down the pit. None of her children would – she would see to that. And, being Eliza, she prevailed after a struggle of wills that lasted for the next two years. Harry pressed the need to earn money, and was countered by Messrs Johnasson and Gordon coming up with both a small pension and a not-too-unhandsome cash tribute. Eliza had arranged her own insurance, and there was quite enough to see the family through.

In due course Harry finished school, and was ordained in 1907 when he was twenty-one years old. He had grown even taller than his father and, in spite of his clerical occupation, more powerful: too tall in fact ever to have managed a working life in the narrow seams of the Durham coalfield. His size and strength, however, stood him in good stead in the early days of his pastoral career. He was first sent to a mission in Liverpool where he comforted the disconsolate, stimulated the lethargic, and quelled the obstreperous with equal success. The Reverend Harold Dickson Ridley was a formidable figure, more than six foot, and fourteen stone in his dog-collar; it took a rash sinner to resist the will of the Lord too stubbornly when Harry was about.

He married a Liverpool girl, but was unable to settle there, being moved about the country every seven years or so, as is the custom with Methodist ministers. It was not until this, his last posting, in 1949, that the Revd Mr Ridley found himself returned to his home county – albeit to Etherley in the hills of West Durham some miles from his native village.

By that time, of course, Eliza was dead. She had gained her point: none of her children had followed their father down the pit, although the Great War had proved equally deadly, claiming two of Harry's brothers. The other siblings had prospered and had left their home ground. Harry was now the only one living in the area.

He had become a man of regular habits, industrious and much respected by all who came into contact with him. The respect was tinged with awe, for even in his late sixties Harry remained a large and powerful man, not given to accommodating himself to sensibilities which he considered over-refined.

After a few days at Etherley he settled into a comfortable routine: he would rise at six every morning and spend an hour at work in his study, before making for his wife the first of the innumerable cups of tea which trickle down the throats of Methodist clergy in the course of a day. After breakfast he would visit the housebound, while afternoons and early evenings were spent in Society meetings. Only the first and last hours of the day could be called his own, and much of those must be dedicated to the preparation of the Sunday services.

Methodists share the same formal liturgy as the Church of England but at that time it was rarely used, the pattern of most services being lessons, a sermon, and hymns. The latter formed a significant part of the service and so choosing the most suitable hymns was an important task: they must complement the sermon and lessons, and some at least must be suitable for hearty congregational singing.

One of the best of these was James Ridley's old favourite, and by no means for the first time Harry found himself humming 'Cwm Rhondda' as, early one morning, he made out his list for the next Sunday's services.

Guide me, O thou Great Redeemer,
Pilgrim through this barren land . . .

It was eminently suitable for the great grey slagheaps, dirty rows of cottages and stunted trees which formed the view from his study window. As he sang through the verses it seemed that the smell of the colliery came back to him as freshly as if he had just come from the mine. Strange, he thought, how the senses could interact so.

As tunes will, the hymn stayed in his head all that morning. It was irritatingly persistent, and Harry attempted to drive it away by playing a few other hymns on the organ – the harmonium that he had inherited from Eliza. But inevitably, whatever tune he started with, after a few bars it modulated into 'Cwm Rhondda'. As he played he became conscious of a presence in the room behind him, and heard, as clearly as if the man himself were there, his father's baritone.

Open now the crystal fountain
Whence the healing streams do flow . . .

The skin on his back went cold: once or twice in the past he had felt compelled to a certain course of action, and had taken this to be the will of God, but never had so powerful an influence wrought upon him. It was no conscious decision of his that brought him to his feet, took him out of the door, and into the car. This was done with some care, for the motor was a pre-war Austin 7, with no superfluous room for one of Harry's size. He knew there was something that must be done, and although he was not yet clear what it was to be, he was confident that instructions would be given in due course.

He drove carefully, as he always did, but quite mechanically across the county, leaving the hills of West Durham for the coastal plain, towards Washington. As he drove his father's voice filled the little car; it carried a message of urgency. '*Let the fiery cloudy pillar Lead me all my journey through* . . .'

It was two in the afternoon when Harry drove through the colliery gates. Everything was changed beyond recognition: the colliery yard was concreted, pithead baths and a canteen had been built, and a new office block replaced the solid red-brick building that had housed the agent and managers. A fresh noticeboard proclaimed that the Usworth Colliery was the Property of the National Coal Board.

Harry entered the office block: it looked more like a hospital than a pit – polished linoleum, light oak desks, coloured photographs, and even some ivy curling up a screen. Had he not been wearing a dog-collar his task might have been harder, but as it was he was taken straight into the manager's office.

The men had changed with the pit: Mr Pennick had always worn solid tweed suits, with a gold watch-chain and high stiff collar; the man who rose to greet Harry, revealed by a name-plate on his desk as Edgar P. Kirkwood, was in shirtsleeves, his collar undone. As the manager looked up at the big old man in clerical clothes, his welcome was civil, though guarded. 'Good afternoon, Reverend. Brenda, could we have a cup of tea? And what can we do for you?'

Harry knew what he had to say but felt that some introduction was needed.

'Mr Kirkwood, what I have to say may sound very untoward and peculiar, but I have good reason for it. Please bear with me.'

The manager looked wary. Clergymen, in his experience,

generally either wanted him to make someone stop doing something, or were after money: he suspected the latter.

'I was brought up in this village as a boy: my father, and his father before him, worked down this pit. You have cousins and nephews of mine here at the moment. I know something of how pits work and what can happen below ground: there are often some pretty odd things among them. My father always used to say you could tell when something was going to go wrong in the mine – there were strange sounds and stillnesses. He thought it might have something to do with the air-pressure changing: at any rate it didn't help him much, for he met his end in an accident here more than half a century ago. What I have come to tell you', and here Harry took a deep breath, 'is that you're going to have a serious accident here any time now.'

Edgar P. Kirkwood was taken aback: he hadn't expected a mad parson. But like most men who have lived with danger he was superstitious and could not brush off such a prophecy.

'Well now, that's something that always might happen. Pits are dangerous places, even with modern equipment. We do everything we can for safety, you know. There's an under-manager who does nothing else, and an area team always making sure we stick to the straight and narrow path.'

Harry saw that this was as far as explanation could go: God would have to take a hand. 'No, Mr Kirkwood, the trouble that I foresee is imminent: it will happen very soon indeed, and will be grave. I must ask you to bring all the men below to the surface now, without delay.'

The man was certainly mad, and Kirkwood was beginning to get annoyed: still, he was a clergyman.

'That's all very well, Reverend, but I can't bring the whole shift to a dead stop just because you fancy there's going to be an accident. There are four hundred men down there, and it would cost thousands of pounds to stop them. No. I'm much obliged for your concern, but I really can't do anything on that evidence. If you're worried, you should write to the Area Safety Officer in Durham.'

'*When I tread the verge of Jordan, Bid my anxious fears subside*.'
The voice echoed in Harry's ears: there was not much time left
and only one solution. He stood up and drew himself to his full
height: the breadth of his shoulders was impressive.

'Mr Kirkwood, I'm sorry to do this, but I know what must be
done, and you must do it.'

He leant over the desk and, seizing the manager with one
hand by the shirt, he dragged him over the top of his own desk.
The stuff of his shirt was too tightly held to let him shout, and
his struggles were ineffective. Harry held him, still in one hand,
up against the wall, his feet six inches off the floor.

'Mr Kirkwood, you will pick up the telephone and instruct
the shift to come to the surface, now. When they are safely here,
you may fetch the police or what you want. But you will get
them up.'

There was nothing Kirkwood could do about it. The man
was homicidal and must be humoured. There was only a couple
of hours left on the shift, anyway, and once he'd got the men up
he'd have this daftie dragged away and locked up.

'All right, then, let me get at the phone.' Harry kept one
massive hand on the manager's shoulder while he telephoned
to the under-manager at the shaft bottom.

'Freddy, look, there's something cropped up. I want you all
up, sharpish. All of you. No, don't argue, just get them all out,
and now.'

He turned to his captor. 'It'll take some time, mind. The face
on the Bustey seam is two miles from the shaft.'

Harry nodded. 'We'll wait, then.'

He should have been horrified at his own actions, and one
corner of his mind was feverishly assessing the consequences –
prison, disgrace, an asylum? But he was possessed of a great
confidence: he had never touched alcohol, but he supposed that
being drunk was something like this.

They waited. After a few minutes the wheels of the lift started
turning as the cage descended, and the first puzzled men, those
who had been working nearer the shaft, blinked in the sunlight.

They stood outside in groups, wondering what was happening. The telephone rang, an angry under-manager wanting to know what the hell he was to do with them.

'Oh, send them home.' Kirkwood looked at Harry. There was something commanding about his quiet certainty. It would do no harm to humour his captor; perhaps there was even something in what the old boy said. 'But keep the rescue teams standing by.'

The two men sat in silence, facing each other across the desk, as the wheels of the lifts rolled and more and more miners poured from the cages and made their way, puzzled, towards the showers. At last the cage came up empty but for two deputies. Harry and Kirkwood looked towards the window and watched them step out of the cage. It came almost immediately: not very dramatic – a tremor of the earth, muffled by more than a thousand feet of rock, followed by a suspiration of dust from the shaft – but quite unmistakably the slight twitch and last breath of a dying mine.

Both men had risen, the manager stunned, Harry elated: he started singing aloud, joining that other voice he could hear, now fading away.

Death of death, and Hell's destruction,
Land me safe on Canaan's side:
Songs of praises
I will ever sing to thee.

He said nothing more, but nodded to the still-speechless manager and walked back to his car through the excited talk of the men in the yard. On the way home he had a tune still persisting in his head, but one with a different lilt to it, a jaunty, swinging rhythm.

Her father loves her well,
Her mother loves her better,
I love the lass mesel'

107

But alas I cannot get her.
Through by the seely side,
Over the moss and the mire,
I'll go to see my lass –
that lives in Hexhamshire,

Hey for the buff and the blue,
Hey for the cap and the feather,
Hey for the bonny lass
That lives in Hexhamshire.

Flodden Field

To those not involved in the educational process, the life of a headmaster of a private school may seem to be leisurely, especially when the school is a relatively small establishment, its pupils young ladies of sixteen or more, and its location a peaceful suburb of Oxford.

The truth, Simon Tate frequently informed his friends, was very different. Terms covered, admittedly, only twenty weeks of the year, and purgatory they were, but much of the rest was occupied in interviewing prospective parents, chasing unwilling parents for unpaid bills, engaging staff, dealing with builders and decorators – the destructive powers of fifty girls were unimaginable – showing oneself at conferences, visiting those schools who sent pupils on to Wyatt House, pleading with universities to accept Sara Miles-Ponsonby on the strength of two indifferent A-levels, and similar unavoidable tasks. Then there was the unmitigated horror of the long vacation term, when the premises were rented to a language school whose pupils infuriated the neighbours, bilked the tradesmen, blocked the sanitary facilities, and complained loudly and endlessly.

True, he generally contrived a trip, together with his wife, to Greece or Egypt before or after Christmas, and perhaps a short motoring holiday in northern France at Easter, but the only time Simon could call his own, and which he cherished accordingly, was the week he spent every September with his friend Hugh Welfare in Northumberland.

They had been up together at the same Oxford college, and had kept in touch thereafter. Hugh had, after a short service-commission in the army, taken over the administration of the family's large, but sparse, estate in Northumberland. The Welfares' lands covered nearly two thousand acres of the River Till valley and its surrounding hills, but only a small part of this was good grazing, the rest becoming pasture of increasing roughness as the hillsides steepened. Properly managed, and all in hand, it provided a decent enough living – especially for a single man.

Hugh had never married, and his easy-going bachelor establishment formed an attractive haven for one who, like Simon, spent his working life surrounded by a monstrous company of females.

September was a good time to visit. The hay harvest had been gathered in, the stock needed only routine attention, and most of the work was on postponable things such as repairing stone dykes and buildings. Although not yet time for the pheasants, there was shooting to be had at rabbits, some duck, and the odd surviving grouse on the hill-tops. It was the season for cub-hunting, which in those parts is an unglamorous but effective affair of long walks with a company of farmers armed with shotguns. Simon was no rider but he liked driving, and Hugh kept a pair of Cleveland Bays with which he had a certain amount of success at trials. With such sports, and a little desultory fishing, Simon had passed several very pleasant holidays, made more enjoyable by the weather. September in the north is often the most agreeable of months.

The two men differed in both character and appearance. Hugh was a solid, quiet, rather sardonic man. Skilled in avoiding the attention of mothers with nubile daughters, permanently tanned by an outdoor life, he found all that he wanted in that part of the country bounded by the rivers Tweed and Tees. He was fond of saying that barbarians began at Berwick and decadence at Darlington, and that anything a man might reasonably require was to be found within eighty miles of Annesley. He would often extol the merits of Newcastle theatres, the Northern Sinfonia, and the beauties of Durham

Cathedral; but, to tell the truth, he very rarely moved much beyond the boundaries of his own estate, except to markets, county shows, and driving trials.

Simon was a much more urban character, enjoying the frequent visits to the opera and theatre that were included in the school's curriculum and well content with the fleshpots of Oxford for most of the year. His visits to Annesley, which he greatly enjoyed, seemed to sharpen his appetite for more sophisticated living. Indeed, for both men, one merit of the time they spent together was the heightened appreciation of their own way of life that their meeting with each other brought.

The September of 1976 began in a similar manner to all those previous Septembers. Simon was met at Berwick station by Hugh driving a Land Rover that smelt strongly of sheep, and they arrived back at Annesley in time for tea, which was a substantial affair with anchovy toast or crumpets, scones and cakes made by Mrs Lowdon, the housekeeper. Hugh kept no servants in the Hall itself. Mrs Lowdon or her daughter came from a cottage on the estate every morning to prepare breakfast, clean and tidy, light the fires, and cook a dinner to which Hugh and his friends would help themselves whenever it seemed convenient to them. Since this was often at a variable time, according to weather and inclination, these meals were always of a kind that would not suffer by being kept waiting.

The day ran true to form: it was too dark after tea to look round the estate, so having bathed and subsequently dealt with Mrs Lowdon's cold grouse and apple pie, the two men sat in front of the library fire, intending to talk. Hugh was feeling sleepy, so, rather than disturb him, Simon took to wandering about the library, idly picking up books here and there. One of these caught his attention, and he began to study it attentively. After a few minutes, seeing that Hugh was not actually asleep, he could not resist addressing him.

'This is a fascinating book. Have you just come across it, or has it been hiding somewhere?'

'How can I tell from here? What is it anyway?' Hugh was very sleepy.

'It's a history of the house and neighbourhood. Very nicely illustrated – about the turn of the century, I think – and with some plans of the house. Do you know, I've never seen a plan of Annesley, except for the drainage layout hanging in your office.'

'Oh, that. It was done for a great-uncle of mine, Walter: he seemed to think the family should have something of a record. Bone up on it, by all means, and you'll know more about the history of Annesley than I do. We're a very dull family: nothing much has ever happened since we finally quietened our northern neighbours up on the hill.'

Simon did in fact take the book to bed, and sat up quite late reading it. Hugh appeared to be right. Since the Battle of Flodden the Welfares had taken no part in any disturbances and made no mark on national life. One forebear had been forced into a Newfoundland baronetcy, but the title died out shortly afterwards: a cousin had been elected as a Radical member in County Durham in the 1860s, but had not contrived to hold his seat for more than eighteen months. And that was that, as far as mentions of Welfares in the nation's annals was concerned: the rest of the book was taken up with descriptions of the estate, nearby places of interest, and, in some detail, the house itself.

Annesley's recorded history began in the twelfth century when a tower was built on the high bank of the River Till to command the crossing. The clifflike banks necessitated a lofty edifice, the foundations of which were in the river bed. The lower half of the tower, some fifty feet or so, clung to the cliff-face before establishing itself on the open ground of the plateau, where the tower proper stood as high again. Since this had been the sole residence of the Welfares until the end of the eighteenth century it had been kept in good repair until that period, and although nothing much had been done to it since then, the solidity of its construction had maintained the fabric relatively intact.

An accession of prosperity, brought about by the Cheviot sheep boom of the time, had led Bartholomew Welfare to build a more elegant residence in the 1780s; he had spared no expense, and engaged Sir James Wyatt to design a splendidly neo-medieval two-storey house, with buttresses, pinnacles, and groin-vaulted hall. Wyatt had agreed to incorporate the original tower in his plan without any alteration other than the addition of some stern machicolations.

Since then the family had lived in Bartholomew's house and had relegated the tower to storage and other ancillary functions.

Annesley must have figured in countless unrecorded Border raids and skirmishes, but is remembered only for the part it played in 1513 during the Battle of Branxton (as the Northumbrians called it) or Flodden, as it became generally known. On 6 September of that year the Scots had actually swept past Annesley, leaving it isolated from the English army. Not being over-anxious for a fight, Annesley's defenders had kept their heads down, and since time had already been lost in capturing Norham, Wark and Etal castles, and perhaps since Annesley was an imposing fortification, the Scots did not waste time in attempting a siege. The Welfares therefore had no part in the battle which took place on the 9th of that month: their opportunity came during the subsequent rout of the Scots.

The fleeing remnants of the Scottish army found their only practicable route was back the way that they had come, down the valley of the river Till: and after the terrible slaughter of the battle it was that way they streamed. The massacre of the battle, and the flight, inspired the grim rhyme:

Tweed says to Till
Why gar ye flow sae still
Till says to Tweed
Although ye run wi' speed
And I run slae
While ye droon ane,
I droon twae.

As soon as they saw the battle was safely won the Welfares left the shelter of Annesley to play their full part in the massacre and looting. There was no question of ransom or surrender, and the river flowed red, inspiring another ballad:

Full mony a soul tae Hell was sped
By the bloody hand of Welfare,
And all the neet the Till flowed red
By the bloody tower of Welfare.

Looking at Annesley today, a picturebook house surrounded by an arboretum planted in 1862 and now at its finest, it was difficult to imagine the scenes of horror and despair that must have taken place there as the terrified fugitives were hacked to pieces.

Simon found the plans reproduced in Uncle Walter's book particularly interesting. They appeared to be Wyatt's original drawings for the new work but included a floor plan of the old tower wing, with a romantic Gothick elevation thrown in for good measure. Simon had never had an opportunity of looking in any detail at the older part of the house, and promised himself a good scramble over it in the morning, with the assistance of the plans.

Hugh's first morning task, which he refused to delegate, had always been to water the horses, and discuss the morning with them. 'Very sensible creatures: never answer back, and say nothing before breakfast. If you could find a woman like that, now, I'd be much inclined to matrimony.' Simon enjoyed these early-morning excursions, and invariably accompanied his friend.

The horses were housed in the ground floor of the old tower only thirty paces from the front door, a position which might not have commended itself to the genteel, but which was accepted as entirely sensible by the Northumbrians. Simon was therefore literally wrong-footed when Hugh turned in the opposite direction and marched off towards the byres and cowshed.

'Oh, I've moved the horses – fitted out some new boxes for them. There's a good deal more light and air than they had before.'

Simon was slightly puzzled by this explanation. The horses had always lived in the tower: he knew Hugh liked having them close at hand, and their new quarters were far enough away to be inconvenient in the long Northumbrian winters.

An advantage of the new arrangement dawned on Simon after breakfast: now that the horses, tack and fodder were cleared out he would have a real chance to examine the old tower and, with the help of the plans, do a little antiquarianizing.

His opportunity came after breakfast when Hugh had to spend some time on his VAT returns. Simon approached his task methodically, starting at the top. The higher storeys were bare of interest, being occupied only by the remains of birds and mice. There was a dusty corridor leading to the Wyatt wing, but no abandoned pieces of antique furniture, ancient artefacts, secret passages or the like; only a great number of empty plastic sacks, much binder twine, rusty corrugated sheeting, and a 1937 Castrol calendar, which he rescued.

The ground floor did present one interesting aspect. On the west wall, the side overlooking the river, he found a dusty door covered for many years by bales of straw but now revealed. It was a very fine door indeed, of oak with overlapping vertical timbers under a four-centred arch, with a magnificent lock, which must, he was sure, be contemporary with the door. The whole was unlikely to be later than the end of the sixteenth century and was far too impressive to be left where it stood. And to what, he wondered, might it lead? There was enough thickness in the wall to allow a staircase, and indeed the plan showed a circular stair at ground-floor level, but there had been no sign of this on the upper floors and, lacking sections, he presumed that any stair must go down towards the river. He would raise the question with Hugh at coffee.

'Oh, that.' Hugh seemed rather taken aback. 'There used to be, ages ago, a way down to the river, when the Till was navigable, but it hasn't been used for ages. It's quite blocked up.'

Simon accepted the rather disappointing news, and since Hugh had finished his paperwork they were able to spend the rest of the week in their customary activities. It was only on the penultimate day of his visit, when Simon was trying his luck with the fish on his own, that he thought he might look at the riverbank under the tower, only a couple of hundred yards downstream. He splashed his way there under the banks which increased in height to form the precipitous cliff on which the tower rested. Sure enough, the square masonry was covered to a height of six feet or more above the water by a mass of boulders and stones swept down in past floods, with shrubs growing from the top of the piles effectively blocking any egress that there might once have been from the tower.

Simon noticed, however, that there were some signs of recent movement: several stones had fallen away, taking the soil with them. It was cold and dark under the shadow of the cliff, and he did not feel much like staying long. He returned to his fishing.

The following day Simon left, taking Uncle Walter's account with him as reading matter for the journey. This proved not without excitement, for he learned that the otherwise un-remarkable Welfares might in fact have that hallmark of an ancient family, a genuine curse! 'Near the west base of Branx-ton Hill in the earlier part of this century a large pit filled with human bones was discovered only some three feet below the surface: the place has been subsequently distinguished by a stone erected by our neighbour, Mr John Collingwood. It is rumoured, and accepted as fact by the older inhabitants of the area, that a much larger inhumation rests where those Scots who fell victim to the swords of the Welfares were thrown, but the whereabouts of this hecatomb has remained a mystery. It appears that some of these unfortunates were alive at the time, and that one wounded Scot pronounced a curse on the family before he was extinguished, to the effect that the line would perish at their hands, although they would have to reach across the centuries so to do. So far, more than three and a half centuries have passed and the Welfares look to have evaded the threat.'

Simon thought nothing more, except that it would make a good story to tell Hugh on his next visit, for he was sure that this history was unknown to him: but on reflection, since Hugh was unmarried and had no close relations – if indeed he had any at all – it might be thought a trifle tactless to mention the possible extinction of the Welfare family.

The autumn term was dissolving in the pre-Christmas festivities when a letter from Hugh arrived. It gave the latest news of the countryside – they'd had some splendid hunting, James Blackett had accidentally shot one of the Duke's guests, Dinah Howard had made off with Tim Stannington, he'd found a promising colt of the Mulgrave stable which he was planning to buy – and ended: 'Why don't you come for New Year? We celebrate it here just as they do in Scotland. Bring Felicity by all means. I would particularly like to see you.'

As it happened they were both able to go, having a few days to spare before leaving on a cruise to the Aegean islands. Hugh was an admirable host: he arranged a suitably lavish and festive luncheon on New Year's Eve, which was followed by a lively party at a country house near Rothbury. Simon noticed, however, that Hugh, for the first time in their long friendship, showed signs of nervousness, particularly at night. He kept glancing into the shadows, and was markedly reluctant ever to go to bed: his complexion was paler, but this might just be the result of the season. Oddly, too, when he was walking around the policies on the morning of their departure, Simon saw that the outer door to the old tower was firmly locked and fitted with an extra padlock, yet, by peering through one of the small windows, he could see that the space beyond was quite empty.

At Easter another invitation came, but Simon could not find the time to visit: he was looking forward to his annual stay in September, but one could have too much of a good thing, and he felt that he needed his taste of France to fortify himself against the impending A-levels.

Hugh was disappointed, and telephoned his friend at the beginning of the summer term to press him to advance his usual visit to the beginning of the long vacation. Simon detected some agitation in Hugh's voice, and agreed to see what he could do.

It turned out to be little enough. There were more than the usual difficulties with the language school: accommodation had to be found at the shortest of notice for an extra fifteen children, in a village where sympathetic prospective landladies were a declining race; the cook had decided to get married, again, and her assistant, who hadn't been married even once, was sunk in gloom, and threatened to leave. It was quite impossible for Simon to get away from the school before the beginning of September, when in response to increasingly insistent and even agitated appeals from Hugh, he arranged to advance his arrival in Northumberland to the 7th of September.

Hugh met him as usual at the station, but it was a very different Hugh. The intervening months had altered the man frightfully: he had lost weight, his healthy complexion had become pale and drawn, and his comfortable taciturnity a febrile loquacity.

'Simon, dear boy, it's very good of you to come. There's no one else I can really talk to about what's been happening. We've had a difficult time with the hay this year – not enough rain at the right time and too much at the wrong. Mrs Lowdon's Cheryl's had another baby: father as usual, we all suppose, but Cheryl isn't sure.'

And so on, with no indication given of what was troubling him. Simon, thinking that it might be a matter of some grave disease, made an enquiry as to his friend's health, but it was brushed aside. 'Oh fine, lost a little weight, but that's no bad thing. I haven't been sleeping so much either.'

The truth came out after supper that night. There had been changes in the domestic arrangements: whereas formerly Hugh had sprawled comfortably all over the house, using one room as a library, another as a gun-room, others as an office, summer smoking-room, company sitting-room, billiard-room, and the like, he had now concentrated all his activities together in one end of the house, that farthest away from the old tower. The two men both ate and sat in the same room, an uncomfortable chamber illuminated by a harsh fluorescent light, cluttered with files, newspapers, and guns. This was another oddity: Hugh had always kept his guns carefully locked away, but now two – a shot-gun and a rifle – were casually laid on a table with packets of cartridges beside them, a form of carelessness un-imaginable in the cautious man he had known.

Hugh fidgeted and poked the fire unnecessarily before beginning.

'Simon, this is serious. I think I may be going mad. No, don't interrupt' – Simon had started to make some anodyne comment and then suddenly reflected that there might be some truth in the statement: too much time spent alone could quite well account for a certain eccentricity. But then, his friend had lived in solitary state for years. Simon sat back in his chair and Hugh continued.

'I've been taking some advice, but the doctors have done nothing for me except give me stupid tablets. You may be able to understand. I'm told it's quite common for people to think they are being followed, pursued, and generally got at – that's what is happening to me, but only in certain places and some times of year. It started a few years back, always at the same season – round about now. I'd be convinced there was someone, or something, after me. I never actually got a fair look at it – it seemed always just on the periphery of my vision, but it was always the same sort of thing – and each year it became a little clearer. It crawled, slithered or hobbled – some uneven movement, as though it wasn't properly put together, or had been badly smashed up. I can hear it too, and it breathes – God – I can hear it, slowly in and out. This goes on for a few days, comes to a sort of climax, and then goes. It's always disappeared by the time you come, and I've felt on top of the world then, as you may have noticed.

'But this last year things changed. It hasn't gone away, and the last few weeks have been terrible. I daren't look round – even now, with you in the room. There aren't any shadows here, I've seen to that; but Christ, Simon – I might see *it* in the full light!

'And it's no use telling me there's nothing there. *You* can't see it, but that proves nothing: it's not interested in you, you don't exist for it and so it doesn't exist for you.

'It has a home, too. Something to do with the tower, behind that door you found. Keeping the horses there must have formed some sort of barrier, sane healthy animals – I wouldn't be surprised if the horses weren't put there for just some such reason. They seem to have been there since about Waterloo, which was soon after Henry Welfare went mad and disappeared. But I had to move them. You remember last year I'd got those new stables when you came? At first I thought they were getting a bit twitchy in the mornings, feed not agreeing with them or something; but then last August, when I came back from Lowther horse-trials, it was a bit late, I was on my own, and I just couldn't get them to go into their boxes. I had to leave them in the field. Then the next night I was passing the tower and heard them stamping about and whinnying, and in the morning they were shaking and sweating as though they were ill. So I moved them up to the byre, a bit warmer there, and had the new stables built.'

Hugh stopped and Simon tried desperately to think of something to say: platitudes about imagining things, needing a rest and such-like, clearly would not do. And it was no good saying that things like this couldn't happen: one had to accept that what went on in a man's mind was the ultimate reality for him. But he tried, anyway.

'What about going away for a time? Leave the whole thing behind?'

'I've thought about it, but this is my home: I'll be damned if I'm going to be driven off by some hobgoblin or other that might just be some chemical misbehaving inside me.'

'I didn't mean going permanently,' Simon responded. 'Just for a month or so – come to Oxford and meet a few new people. You never see anyone here you haven't known for ages. And remember Oscar Wilde – "In a crisis, presence of mind is less important than absence of body."'

Hugh smiled for the first time. 'Perhaps you're right. I'll think seriously about it, at any rate. It's very good for me to have you here.'

Shortly afterwards they retired. Their bedrooms adjoined, with a connecting door, and Simon could see that the light in the next room was not switched off.

Hugh did seem improved in spirits on the next day, market day in Wooler, to which he drove with a load of that season's lambs. Simon preferred to stay at home: he felt that a little poking around might be in order.

The door to the tower was still locked, and, peering through the window, he thought that everything inside seemed untouched, with the mysterious old door firmly shut.

He decided to reconnoitre the river end, and scrambled down the bank some distance from the tower where the going was a little easier. As he approached the place where the tower foundations joined the stream, he saw that there had been a considerable change. The boulders that had formerly hidden the base had been swept or taken away, and the shrubs with their retaining earth had also disappeared. The masonry of the old tower was now exposed all the way to the river; it seemed probable if an exit from the tower had ever existed, it might now be visible not far below the surface of the water. The temptation to examine more closely was strong, but as Simon, not without some trepidation, advanced he slipped and fell. The water was very cold, and he had some difficulty in regaining his balance. His curiosity dampened with the rest of him, Simon turned back to the house: it really was very dark and unpleasant in the shadow of the tower, and the river smelt damnably of something foul and decomposing – dead sheep, most likely.

Hugh, on his return at teatime, was much improved. 'Simon old chap, I'm going to take your advice. Just going to market made a difference – all the chattering and those healthy uncomplicated people. We'll travel together when you're ready to go back, if that's all right by you? There are only a few things I need to clear up before I leave.'

One of these things seemed to involve building, since Simon saw that Hugh had brought a load of bricks and cement back from Wooler, which had been stacked outside the tower.

That evening was a much more comfortable affair: they made plans for what should be done at Oxford; perhaps a weekend in London might be arranged. They speculated as to the fates of some of their contemporaries: Derek Studely-Smith was a successful publisher, but his inseparable friend Madgely had disappeared without trace. Did anyone ever read any of Freddy Gorin's books? Hugh seemed much calmer when they retired, but Simon could not help noticing that the light in the next door room was still allowed to burn all night.

The following day, 9 September as it happened, they spent the morning trying to clear the woods of rabbits. Hugh was quite his old self again, and shot extremely well. Simon kept his end up, with the result that they were forced to leave some of their bag behind for later collection; they contrived to finish at the Black Swan for a late ham sandwich and beer, having covered a good fourteen miles.

Expansive over the second pint, the two men enlarged on their plans for amusements in Oxford. 'There's only one thing that must be done before we leave,' said Hugh, 'and then I'll be able to go with a quiet mind. It won't take long, and we should be able to catch the 12.50 tomorrow.'

'Anything I can help with?' Simon volunteered.

'Not really, old chap. This is something I've got to do myself, I fancy,' Hugh answered, but did not explain further.

Simon found on their return that the unaccustomed exercise, and Mrs Lowdon's tea, induced a comfortable somnolence which he indulged by retiring to his bedroom and falling asleep.

It was after seven when he awoke, feeling, rather surprisingly, quite hungry. He decided to rout Hugh out and suggest dinner. Hugh was not to be found in his room, nor in the only room that was currently in use downstairs. Nor was there any message from him, as might have been expected had he been called away. Although it was almost too dark outside to make anything more than a cursory search, Simon found a torch and set out. At the door he paused: he felt certain, horribly certain, he knew where Hugh had gone, and he took a heavy blackthorn from the umbrella stand.

The outer door of the tower was open and the lights were on. Some cement had been mixed and the bricks brought inside on a wheelbarrow. Three or four courses had already been laid around the strange door that led to the mysterious staircase, apparently in an effort to block up that opening permanently.

And the door was standing open. Grasping the stick firmly Simon stepped over the bricks and shone the light through the open doorway. There was indeed, as he had speculated, a staircase, a circular stone affair such as one sees in Norman keeps, leading down. What could be seen of the walls and treads was covered with grey slime and mould, and a nauseating odour drifted out. The place was redolent of horror, and nothing, absolutely nothing, would have persuaded Simon to advance a step further.

With a good deal of common sense, if not much courage, he dashed back into the house and telephoned for the police. They arrived very quickly indeed – police in that part of the country have little to do, and spend most of their time waiting for something to happen – a sergeant and a constable, properly equipped with ropes and lights. Even so, it was difficult to

123

negotiate the staircase safely, for a firm footing on the slippery treads was impossible and the constable who went down did so with the help of a rope belayed round one of the stalls.

Simon and the sergeant waited apprehensively on the threshold until, after quarter of an hour, the constable emerged, wet, filthy, and gasping for breath.

'Useless, the whole of the bottom of the stairway is under water . . . There's a tangle of things down there I can't rightly make out . . . we'll have to send for the frogmen.'

This was done, again with commendable speed. In the short interval before their arrival Simon plucked up courage to examine the top of the staircase, near the doorway. What he found there made him shiver with horror, but he kept his discovery to himself. When the divers and the ambulance arrived with all their equipment there was so much bustle that Simon had an opportunity to recover himself. What he had seen was soon eradicated in the bustle and commotion, and nobody asked Simon questions he would have preferred not to answer.

The frogmen were eventually successful. The inspector in charge approached Simon. 'I'm afraid they found Mr Welfare, sir. He must have slipped and fallen down. They're bringing him up now, and we'll take him straight to Rothbury. There's no need for you to be here, sir. It can't be very pleasant. But we'd be obliged if you could spare a few minutes in the morning.'

Simon was duly grateful. He felt he could not possibly spend the night alone in the house, and telephoned to arrange a room in a Wooler hotel.

He slept badly, and was at the police station first thing next morning.

'It's much as we thought, Mr Tate,' the inspector explained. 'It must be forty feet down to the bottom of the staircase, and he'd gone all the way. Which is a bit curious when you come to think of it, for you'd expect a falling body to get wedged in one of the curves of the stair.'

'Was he badly – knocked about?' asked Simon.

'Just as you might expect,' the inspector answered. 'He'd struck his head in falling, and broken a good number of bones – I'm sorry to say, sir, but you did ask.' Simon was looking pale. There was one question he wanted to ask, but did not dare. The inspector continued. 'You told us that the door had been locked for years, which is just as well. Mr Welfare wasn't the first down there, by any means. We found a lot of mud and roots at the bottom, and stuck among them scores of bones – human bones – and bits of what seem to have been weapons or armour. Nothing for us to worry about, for they've obviously been there for hundreds of years, but we'll have to make sure they're properly buried. They're still bringing them out this morning.

'And, which is also odd, there was a way right through to the river, where we found a lot more bones – sheep mainly and a fair bit more recent. Almost as though something had been living there. An otter you might say, but I've never heard of otters eating sheep. Well, we've got enough to worry about as it is, and it's always been a queer sort of river, the Till. I keep well away from it myself.'

Simon did not tell him (nor did he ever make any reference to the subject thereafter) exactly how queer it was.

When he had summoned up his courage to look through the doorway the night before he had seen two things the police had not noticed. One was that a brick had been shattered as though – and he did not like to dwell on it – someone had tried to defend himself with the only weapon near to hand.

The other was that on the wall of the stair, incised through the slime into the stone itself, were the marks of fingers, desperately clawing at the wall as if in a vain attempt to stop being dragged down to a vile death. The question he had wanted to ask was whether there had been injuries to Hugh's hands: a positive answer would have only confirmed his terrible theory, and he dreaded that happening.

And what would he have found if he could have brought himself to examine the broken brick? Hair, but of what? Scales, perhaps? Hugh was dead, by whatever means, and who could know into what dark realms the answers to such questions might lead?

The new wing

King James I of Scotland was a man bloody, bold and resolute, his temper toughened by twenty years' imprisonment in England, and suited to the stark and desperate times in which he lived. One of his more famous escapades is still well known on the Borders, although the passage of time sometimes leads to its being attributed to James I of England, more than a century and a half later. This was the suppression of the cruel band of murderers and cannibals known as the Sawney Beans, after the leader of the tribe. Originally a tinker, Bean had, in the disturbed years after the Black Death, set up as a footpad in the old Kingdom of Galloway. His success attracted to him other criminals of both sexes, who, together with his own family, prospered in their vile trade. Although many attempts were made to root them out, all failed, since the Sawneys had discovered an impregnable refuge in one of the sea caves of that coast, not far from Ballantrae.

In time new generations were born, debased and savage creatures, the product of incest; and driven by hunger they took to cannibalism. The bodies of slain travellers were no longer found, except perhaps in time of plenty, when only the tenderest morsels – livers, kidneys, sweetbreads and buttocks – would be taken, leaving the mangled carcase as a testimony to the fact that the Beans were not extinct. Old Sawney held a despotic sway, taking what women he chose: those who attempted to dispute his rule were summarily dispatched and eaten.

These depredations became so notorious and unsettling to the peace of the kingdom that King James himself had to assemble a strong company. Aided by bloodhounds, the royal troops found the hidden refuge, and on entering even those hard men were horrified by what they discovered. The Beans had become entirely animal and degenerate; they were naked, pallid in the dim light of the cave, the floor of which was strewn with human bones and fragments of decaying flesh. Fresher bodies hung in a sort of game larder to await their coming to the desirable degree of putrefaction.

The creatures put up a desperate resistance, and those that survived were taken to Glasgow. The men were emasculated, their hands and feet struck off, and were left to bleed to death; the women were burned alive. The word 'Sawney', a 'derisive term for Scotchman' as the Oxford English Dictionary has it, has lingered in the language, although few recall the derivation of the word. The cave, purified by the passage of centuries, can be seen by arrangement with the local council.

This brief historical note may, or may not, have something to do with the mysterious and unpleasant story that follows: the reader should form his own judgement.

In all places and at all times man has needed special skills to prosper. In more straightforward – let us not say primitive – societies these are primarily those of physical strength, speed and dexterity. While such basic qualities are still useful, more sophisticated arts have become necessary, especially for those living in great cities. How, for example, to deal with police and head-waiters (both should be approached with a similar blend of affability and condescension); how to procure the least uncomfortable seats on aeroplanes; how to find the lavatories in the Houses of Parliament; how to get out of London at weekends.

Ralph Gillett was adept and a past master at all such man-oeuvres, but even experts err. Old Henry had come to luncheon, and come early: there was nothing for it but to be civil and feed the old boy everything from dry sherry to kümmel: after all, he had been senior partner for two decades and had a right to expect civility in exchange for the power he had surrendered. Such work as Ralph had to finish that afternoon before the long weekend was rushed off in a slapdash way, his secretary Claire in a rebellious mood and determined to make some startling error, just to show him!

And then some idiot had blocked him into the underground garage. The head porter had to search for the offender, who proved to be a client; more civility was proffered, by now wearing a little threadbare. And then it was 3.40, and it is a truth universally acknowledged in the City of London that half-past three is the latest possible time by which to leave on a Friday afternoon.

Nevertheless Ralph felt that he might just succeed by using little-known short cuts through Islington, Camden and Primrose Hill. He was stopped for ten minutes in Upper Street, listening to the LBC traffic programme warning him of congestion in Upper Street, and found an impassable jam behind Euston, which turned out to be an American tourist's car sandwiched between a lorry and a lamp-post. When five o'clock found him still in Hendon, he accepted the need to revise his schedule. He was due to arrive in Westmorland at 7.30, but there was no prospect, however well things might go on the motorway, of now getting there much before nine.

Things did not go well, so that around half-past seven Ralph telephoned from a convenient service area to make his excuses. It was not, thank heaven, going to be a formal weekend: few things were formal in Westmorland. There was to be a recital, due to start shortly while he was still a hundred-odd miles away, and he would not be missed among the crowd of people that would be present. As the music was to be provided by a wind ensemble – a demanding prospect after a long Friday night drive – he did not feel too many regrets at his inevitable absence; still, he felt it only right, for he was a man conscious of his obligations, to warn his hostess of his late arrival.

He did not in fact manage to speak to her, since she was about her social duties, but left an appropriately contrite message with one of the children, or one of the childrens' legion of friends, refreshed himself with Lord Forte's coffee, and resumed his journey.

The traffic had become easier, and having salved his conscience, Ralph was in a more relaxed frame of mind. From Preston the road became a positive enjoyment, and the final descent through the Lune Gorge, flanked by silent hills, was as dramatic and inspiring as ever.

He left the motorway at Tebay to take the last few miles of country road. In doing this he was following one of the most ancient routes in the island: the Maiden Way, old before the Romans made it their military road to the Wall, the only practicable one on the West of the Pennines. It remained so throughout the Dark Ages and thereafter, until a new road over Shap was made in the eighteenth century, where now the railway and motorway follow.

Orton Scar, the watershed between Lune and Eden, provides a sharp demarcation between the placid north of England and the wilder and more savage Borders. Beyond this, every town has its castle, every village its pele tower, and memories of terror and bloodshed have soaked into the land. As Ralph crossed the highest point he could see standing stones silhouetted against the night sky, a threat and a warning. The whole Scar was littered with such remains. It is always difficult to traverse that bleak moor without a shudder, and it is certainly no place in which to find oneself alone at night. The rapid transition from this sad and lonely spot to the quiet valley of the Lyvennet is a relief, and it was with that profound emotion, possibly also influenced by the end of his 280-mile drive, that Ralph approached his destination.

Ravenswood was a large house by any standards, and very large by the modest ones of Cumbria, but was so well placed and screened by great trees as to be invisible until the pillars of the gates were passed, when its grey bulk appeared with startling suddenness.

The carriage drive was full of cars whose owners had come for the concert and stayed for supper, but Ralph knew that a coach house would have been kept empty for his car. He drove to it, parked the car with an affectionate pat, and began the walk back to the house. It was almost entirely dark, with just enough light to distinguish the gap between the trees where the road lay. The trees crowded in on both sides oppressively, and as he walked carefully forward he heard rustlings among the shrubs. Pheasants – or something in search of pheasants? There was also an odd smell. But the countryside is an insanitary place.

The house lights, as Ralph approached, revealed nothing but the expected motor cars. He walked in, down the flight of stone steps to the upper hall, and down more stairs to the central hall under the glass dome, full of bustle and sociable conversation. The light and happy noise were a welcome contrast to the dark and silent – or almost silent – night outside.

The concert had finished, players and audience had eaten, although some of the horns were still at the ham, it being in the nature of horns to be hungry. Everyone else was drinking – it was a house where the drink rarely ran out – and beginning some desultory dancing. Ralph smiled around generally, hoping that this would encompass anyone he might know but did not recognize, and moved in search of his hostess. He found Flora coping with the contra-bassoon, always a boisterous instrument: she was flatteringly pleased to see him, although this may have in part been due to gratitude at having been rescued from the thirsty and amorous contra-bassoon.

'Dear heart' – Flora, who could never remember even her closest friends' names reliably, was given to such affectionate generalities – 'how absolutely splendid to see you! So good of you to come all this way. Do help yourself to beer (this is to the contra-bassoon), you'll find it in the butler's pantry.'

'I'm very much looking forward to a country weekend. We lead such quiet lives in London, compared with the permanent excitement that goes on up here.' Ralph was not being ironic: Flora's weekends were characterized by constant activity. 'But

I think you've got a prowler outside. I'm sure I heard something in the bushes. Do you think the cars are safe?'

'Oh, we can't worry about them; people round here don't go in for stealing, anyway. They'll cheat each other terribly, and poach unmercifully, but not actually pinch things from cars. It was probably only some village lads seeing what's going on. Now you've missed a super concert, but I think they're going to start again any minute, and they're better when they've had a drink. Here, quick, have a whisky to catch up.' She seized a not-too-dirty glass – one did not expect clean glasses at Ravenswood, at that time of night – and poured a sextuple whisky. 'Look, the food's all been cleared away, but there's some left for you, I know. I put some salmon on a plate when I heard you were going to be late, and there's salad, and trifle, and things. It's in the big fridge in the end room in the new wing – you know where that is – do go and help yourself, and hurry back.'

Ralph smiled; he would enjoy quietly eating in the kitchen where he could catch up on the village gossip from the girls who had come to help. So, sipping his whisky, he worked his way back through the hall, down the library corridor, through the baize door, past the butler's pantry, the larder, the dairy, the game larder, the preparation room, and out into the kitchen court. The new wing lay on the other side of the court, a single-storey building of intercommunicating rooms with the more modern pieces of equipment – washing-machines, rotary irons, deep-freezers, and refrigerators – housed in suitable conditions.

He opened the outer door and felt for the light switch: no light was forthcoming. A failed bulb? They had once tried to count the exact number of bulbs in the house and had got to 270 when disputes broke out as to whether there were two or three in the upper tower room, or any at all in the apple room, which nobody felt inclined to confirm. It was hardly unusual for some of them, at least, to be inoperative. There was quite enough light, anyway, coming from the kitchen court to make progress

132

easy, so Ralph advanced to the next door in line. Once again there was no light, but, no matter, the illumination was still enough to open the next door, and the next, to find the big refrigerator, and to discover it to be quite innocent of food although harbouring a number of bottles of champagne.

He smiled again – just like Flora, who never got things quite right. At any rate he would not die of thirst, and there was sure to be some ham left. He took a bottle and turned back, to find facing him at the end of the corridor, and indistinctly outlined against the courtyard light, two small figures.

It was too dark to recognize them; they were short enough to be children, but squat and oddly shaped. Flora often had handicapped children to stay: were these perhaps Downs Syndrome children, Mongols? As he worked his way along the wall towards them he felt they were not; they really were misshapen, almost ape-like, and gave off a most offensive smell. But some of Flora's guests were very odd indeed. Ralph felt unaccustomedly awkward, and even a little nervous.

'I'm afraid there's nothing to eat along here,' he said, in a somewhat light-hearted fashion.

He was wrong.

It was some time before Flora remembered Ralph, after the party had thinned out considerably. There were a good number of places he might have been, but as the house guests drifted into the library, the customary refuge and meeting-place before bed, it was clear that he had gone missing. Flora slipped away herself to look in some bedrooms, and noticed that his bag had been left on the stairs where he had put it down as he came in. She was a little perturbed, and organized a general search.

The young man who had been detailed to investigate the kitchen quarters came back looking pale and disturbed, finding some difficulty in his speech.

'Look, Flora, I'm afraid something must have happened. I

133

can't see terribly well, the lights seem to have fused, but something's wrong. There's a terrible smell, and I think . . . well, I think there's some blood . . . quite a lot, in fact.'

Flora was not one to panic, and bulbs were found. One of the soberer men put together a gun, and the whole party, nobody being very keen on remaining by themselves, went to look.

There was not much to see. No sign of Ralph, or anyone else. But at one point there had been a great deal of blood splashed about, splashed vigorously, rather as a rumbustious bather might splash water. Rather horribly, the wall, which seemed to have been covered with blood, had been wiped, or possibly even licked, clean to a height of four feet or so. There was also a broken champagne bottle, with some strands of very coarse sandy hair adhering to it.

The police dogs, who came quickly enough, were able to follow a track, for there were bloodstains and fragments of cloth. It led them for a hundred yards, as far as the river. From there any traces there might have been were washed away downstream.

Neither then, nor later was any satisfactory explanation provided for this tragedy. I have my own idea, which the introduction to this story may have suggested. To support this, I would mention that the river Lyvennet, where the dogs lost the scent, flows via the Eden to the Solway Firth, on the other side of which are the hills of Galloway. We are told that the Sawney Beans were extirpated by James I, but we cannot be sure that some did not escape. If they had done so, one must wonder to what would four more centuries of cannibalism and in-breeding have reduced them?

And three more facts. First, the new wing at Ravenswood was built on the site of the oldest part of the house, which dated from the Middle Ages. If there were, or are, such creatures, it is that place, to which the ancient routes ran, that would have been imprinted on their folk memory.

Secondly, the hair on the champagne bottle was human, which disposed of any theory of an animal attack.

Finally, not far away a ruined cottage stands on a deserted road known as 'Bloody Bones Lane'. No cogent reason has been advanced as to how it came by this unpleasant designation.

An everyday story of country folk

The doors of the Cross Keys opened at six every weekday evening. The only exceptions were the annual show day, and perhaps at such festive occasions as Boxing Day when the shooters would usually linger until nearly five, after which a publican had to have some rest. No later than ten past six Taylor Thomson would arrive with his dog, and begin on the first of his two half-pints. Taylor had retired after a tediously undistinguished career in local government and, finding time hanging heavily upon his hands, could be relied upon for one and a half hours every evening, when by virtue of being first he commandeered the most comfortable chair.

The identity of the next visitor could not be predicted. For the following hour the bar would be the preserve of the salaried or quasi-gentrified class. It was, as Joe Finlay had worked out shortly after taking over the Cross Keys, a question of eating-habits. The farmers and labourers took a substantial meal after milking was over, and by seven or so were ready for a pint and a chat before settling indoors for the night. The later-dinner brigade, who ate at eight o'clock, felt sociably thirsty before that time and were likely to be on parade at opening time. After nine-thirty or so the field was open and anybody might turn up.

On that particular autumn evening the pattern was broken. True, Taylor was in his habitual chair when Tom Faulkner the auctioneer dropped in at 6.20 on his way home, which was usual enough; but within a few minutes Stan Gibson erupted into the bar. Old Stan was the cowman over at the Grange, a man who liked a bit of gossip, just as they all did to be sure, but was as set in his habits as any man in the parish. He should have been nicely finishing off his tea at this hour, not bursting into the pub, and from the bits of cream on his whiskers it was obvious that he had bolted his meal and come hot-foot to the Cross Keys.

'Why Stan, what's up wi' thee?' Joe asked, inadvertently imitating the accent of his customer. It was a habit he could not break, and it had stood him in good stead in his former career as a teacher of French to unwilling middle-school children.

'There's nowt up wi' me, lad. Ye should be askin what's up w' Lance Wharton ower at t'Hall. Gie us a pint, lad, quick.'

'All right Stan, what's up with Lance then?' Tom Faulkner asked obligingly, while Joe drew the beer. 'Has he found another lady, or bought another Mercedes, or fallen into the slurry pit?'

Stan took a deep draught of his beer. 'Nay, nay, nowt like that. Only the last of them would be news, like. Nay, he's gan to plough up t'Hall Bottom. Hoo's that, then!'

His listeners did not show the astonishment that Stan obviously expected from them. Neither Taylor nor the landlord were sure why this should be regarded as so startling a piece of news. Tom Faulkner, who knew all about the farms nearby, was better informed. 'That's always been permanent pasture, hasn't it? It's a shame to plough anything as old as that; but it's good bottom land, so I can see the argument for it.'

Westmorland farms all follow a similar pattern: a share of good, relatively low-lying land near the village, including a garth round the house; meadows and pasture on the lower slopes of the hills; and either an allotment or a stint on the fells for summer grazing. Most of all this is grass, and whatever is put down for feed is generally on the bottom land, where barley and swedes are sometimes grown. This being so, it hardly seemed unreasonable that a decent bit of land should be proposed for that purpose.

A thought struck Taylor. 'There's a right-of-way across Hall Bottom, isn't there? Is that what's worrying you, Stan?' Stan was too busy with finishing his beer to comment, and Taylor continued. 'But it would be diverted round the edge of the field. That's not unreasonable, surely?'

Stan's pint was finished, but it had not assuaged his indignation.

'You don't know nowt, none o' you know, do you? That's nay any owd path, that yon. That's t'owd Corpse Road. Bin there sin afore Lord knas whin. He canna gae round disturbing yon.'

Light dawned in varying degrees in the smoke-filled atmosphere, smoke not only from pipes and cigarettes, but also from the fire. Nothing that Joe could do would prevent it smoking when the wind was in the east. He went over to the fire to adjust the logs. 'I still don't see why you are so alarmed, Stan.'

Taylor explained. 'Stan is quite right. You'll find a corpse road in most of the big parishes round about here. There's a well-known one over by Haweswater marked on the Ordnance Survey map. They go right back to the Dark Ages. The idea was that whenever anyone died at an outlying farm and had to be brought to the churchyard for burial, which was often a long way, they should go along the same path.'

Tom Faulkner added, 'You can trace the road from the churchyard right up to the high fell. It runs along the water-meadows, then over a stile, across Hall Bottom, and by the Hall, then goes pretty straight from farm to farm up the dale and to Beck Head, which is the last farm before the fell top.'

'And you know what superstitions are,' Taylor continued. 'Over the centuries the paths became taboo, like the churchyard itself. All that road is still looked on as a sort of consecrated ground by some of the oldsters.'

'A don't know about "superstitions" or "the oldsters" – we know more than we get credit for. Give us a pint, Joe. A wouldn't disturb a corpse road, that's certain, neither would owd Wilkie Milburn, when he built t'new Hall.'

The auctioneer whistled. 'So that's why there's a tunnel there.' He turned to Joe and Taylor. 'You remember, where the path runs by the Hall? It's only a few yards from the house itself, and you'd have expected it to have shifted when they built the new Hall last century. Nobody wants a public right-of-way just outside their front door. But they did no such thing, just dug that tunnel you have to go through. Must have cost a mint, even then. Wilkie Milburn wasn't going to disturb the corpse road, and he was a mean old blighter from all accounts.'

'Nae more would Lance Wharton, if he'd got any sense at all,' Old Stan grunted, attacking his second pint.

The subject was left there for the moment, but by closing time the news was round the village. It had reached even the vicarage (always the last place to hear any gossip) as early as breakfast time the next day, brought along with the newspaper by Miss Furness from the shop.

'Oh dear, we've got another village row on our hands,' Mrs Frankland exclaimed, handing *The Times* to her husband. The Revd Mr Frankland was reluctant to let anything interfere with the newspaper, but knew his duty. He laid it down with only a small sigh, and was given the story of Lance Wharton's intention to plough up Hall Bottom.

'It does seem a pity to interfere with permanent pasture, but we should really hear Lance's side of the story first, don't you think?' He felt rather pleased with this conclusion, which sounded even-handed and responsible while, more important-ly, allowing him to get on with his toast and *The Times*.

He was not given a long remission, for hardly had he started the crossword than the telephone rang. It was Mrs Lamb, well known for her conservationist enthusiasms, complaining about the threatened destruction of innumerable botanical varieties for which the Hall Bottom was apparently famous. When she had been succeeded by Ian Hibbard, representing the Ramb-lers' Association, by the local newspaper, and the Country Landowners' Association, Frankland realized that he could not avoid at least raising the question with Lance Wharton, although he did not expect much success from it.

Wharton was one of the new generation of farmers who had

found themselves able to make a great deal of money as tenants. With land worth £2,000 an acre and upwards, making the minimum viable farm worth half a million or so, owning land was not nearly so good a proposition as renting it, since rents were strictly controlled. Lance, like his father before him, had a tenancy of the Standale Hall home farm, locally known as the Grange. Standale New Hall, built in the last century, was uninhabited and ruinous, but the Grange and its buildings, only a couple of hundred yards away, were well kept up. If Lance was not a good farmer in every sense of the word – he was impatient with stock, and over-lavish with pesticides and ferti- lizers – he was dedicated to, and efficient at, making money.

He worked hard, and got hard work from his labourers. Holidays were rare and profits went mainly into expensive machinery and a new car every year, thus rescuing considerable amounts from the hands of the tax collector. Lance's only respectable diversion was shooting, and even this was turned into a commercial activity since he had recently acquired shooting rights to a large tract and had set up rearing-pens and feeding-tubs preparatory to syndicating the shoot. A few dozen poults had been put down that year, but next season was to be on an altogether grander scale.

The vicar chose his time and dropped in at the Hall as tea was being set. This was the light meal – sandwiches, bread and cheese, scones and cakes – taken at about 3.30 before milking, as opposed to high tea or supper after milking was done.

As he had feared, Lance proved unreceptive. 'Everyone will tell you it's too good a bit of land to let go on as pasture. There's no subsidy on the low land and I can get a good yield of barley, which is doing well just now. Besides, I could do with some more feed for the pheasants – it makes good cover for the poults too.

'And there's no case to make about the right-of-way. There's plenty of room at the edge. You can be sure some of those Rambler dafties'll walk through the middle anyway, and I can't stop them.'

The vicar tried, as delicately as might be, to hint at the superstitions about the old corpse road.

'Why, I'm surprised at you listening to all those old women's mitherings, vicar. Farming's a modern industry nowadays, the biggest i' the country; it'd be a bad job if we let ourselves be ruled by a lot of silly stories.'

And that was that. There was a good deal of fuss, including correspondence in the newspaper, which Lance ignored. His landlord, the Earl of Scourbridge, was approached, but the agent explained quite reasonably that a landlord had little power to interfere in what a tenant did, provided he behaved responsibly, and that Mr Wharton's proposals could not seriously be called irresponsible.

As October approached and the land was due to be ploughed, Stan developed severe arthritis and had to take a week off work. Lance could not decide whether this was a genuine illness or malingering, although there was the doctor's certificate to back it up. Lance knew well that his hinds were reluctant to plough Hall Bottom and that Stan was more vociferous than most on the subject. It therefore fell to Lance himself to do the ploughing, a task he rather enjoyed. With his latest massive tractor and ploughshare the work was soon done, the pale green late grass turning strip by strip to a rich brown, the old track completely obliterated.

Refreshed by his day in the open air he decided that he would pay a visit to the Cross Keys after supper. He did not often go there, preferring a grander establishment in Penrith where he might drink champagne cocktails unobserved by the critical eyes of his neighbours, but this evening he was too tired to face the drive. Besides, he might even find Stan at the Cross Keys, instead of in bed where he was supposed to be. Best of all, he would show up their silly superstitions: he had ploughed up the old corpse road and no harm had come to him.

'Hello, Lance, had a good long day's ploughing?' said Joe, greeting him as he came into the rosy glow of the bar.

Everyone turned round and eyed him. 'Aye thanks, but it's thirsty work – let's have a pint of the best, please.'

'Everything's best in here,' said George Turnbull, another of Lance's farm-hands, offering him a bar stool, the only seat left. Lance sat down.

'How are the pheasants getting on?' asked Joe.

'Oh, they seem to be doing very well. We won't start shooting till the middle of November, though. Give them time to fatten up a bit on the berries.'

The evening passed pleasantly enough, and no one mentioned the corpse road, nor did Stan turn up to cast a gloom. Lance felt pleased that he had gone to his local and, in some measure, made peace with his critics. Although by closing time he had taken a few pints of the best, on leaving he managed to walk steadily enough to the car and climb in. He turned the ignition key, but nothing happened. He looked down the silent street. There was no one about. Half cross that he could not hail anyone to give him a push, and half pleased that his expensive car's failure would not be observed, he decided to walk home, persuade his wife to return with him in the other car, and tow him back.

The quickest way home was, of course, along the old corpse road. Taking from the car the powerful torch used for searching out night-time lambs, Lance set off over the fields. He enjoyed walking in the darkness, as the moon came through the breaks in the clouds and rabbits scurried away from the light of his torch – until he crossed the stile into Hall Bottom and realized he would have to walk round the edge of the field rather than straight across on the vanished path. He cursed, then grinned at the thought that he was the first person to be inconvenienced by his own ploughing. The trees along the edge of the field moaned as their branches moved in the breeze, an uncanny sound. It was striking cold, and he had no overcoat; the going round the broken headlands was hard, but he began to improve his pace, and finally to run. It was only to keep warm, he reassured himself, but he could not escape a growing conviction that something was following him; he did not care to turn and see if that was so. By the time he gained the welcome warmth and light of his own kitchen he was quite out of breath, snapped at his wife, and decided to postpone the retrieval of his car until the following morning. When the time came to do so, the car, inexplicably enough, started immediately. Lance concluded that he must have been drunker than he had imagined, and quickly forgot the whole incident.

When Stan returned from his bout of illness and found Hall Bottom ploughed he said nothing, but his wrath moved through gloom to a ghoulish expectation of terrible consequences. Since accidents were not unusual – the countryside being a much more dangerous place than town dwellers imagine – it was not surprising that old Stan was soon given some cause for satisfaction. It was a common enough occurrence, and no one was actually harmed, but it could hardly be denied that the circumstances were significant.

Lance had been out shooting with a friend: they were climbing the stile leading from the meadow into Hall Bottom when his friend's gun discharged. He had been about to break it before negotiating the obstacle, but his fingers slipped, and the piece went off. Since he had prudently kept the barrels pointing down, the shot went harmlessly into the ground, but it was very near to Lance's foot, near enough to give him a nasty shock.

Nothing to it you might say, but Stan hammered the point that the accident had taken place on the corpse road itself, right next to the ploughed field. 'If that's nae warning, I'm a Dutchman. Wait an' see what comes next, that's all.'

It proved a disappointing winter from that point of view. Lance Wharton's fortunes continued to flourish. The spring brought a successful lambing and the new barley in Hall Bottom came along well. There was no noticeable sign of any retribution for disturbing the dead.

Stan might have been happier had he known more. The incident with the gun had in fact disturbed Lance considerably – and not unnaturally, for coming so near to having one's foot blown off is an upsetting event. And, unknown to Stan, it had been followed by others.

These started again in January, when a thaw had set in. Noises can be expected during a thaw – snow falling from eaves and branches, water trickling, becks rushing, cold metal expanding in the winter sunshine – but these were peculiar noises. Scurryings like animals in the undergrowth, but in places where there was no undergrowth. Whistles and screams which could have been foxes or owls, but coming from spots where foxes and owls rarely ventured, and in daylight. Nothing absolutely inexplicable, but certainly and unpleasantly odd.

A peak was reached in the dark February nights, when the happenings seemed at their worst around the tunnel where the old corpse road ran past the Hall. It was never a cheery place; the path had been sunk well below the surface of the ground before the tunnel proper began, and was overshadowed by an avenue of desolate yew overtopped by elms. Generations of leaves and branches lay underfoot, raising susurrations and crackling noises as one passed. The walls of the tunnel were permanently damp, with water dripping slowly down from the vaulted roof.

Lance took to hurrying along through the passage when occasion had him there after dark, and to carrying a stick and a torch. Even the torch was a mixed blessing, for he became uncertain of what it might illuminate, afraid of pointing the light into the dark places for fear of what he might glimpse there. After a time he kept the torch firmly shining on the ground immediately in front of him, and never, for any reason, ever so much as glanced back over his shoulder.

With the spring and lighter nights the noises ceased and Lance's spirits improved. The tales people put around were enough to scare anyone, he concluded, at least when the nights were long. Some protective instinct, however, led him to avoid using the tunnel whenever possible, which the improved weather made easier to do.

He was busy about the farm and had little further leisure to speculate about the matters which had, just a few weeks before, so depressed and frightened him. Human beings are resilient: when one has a bad cold it is impossible to imagine life without its misery, but as soon as it goes all the discomfort is forgotten. Perhaps another incident should have warned Lance all was not well. He was driving down Quarry hill one night in April when there was a sharp late frost, a thing much dreaded by farmers in lambing-time, following a day of rain. Suddenly he saw head-lights coming fast round the hairpin bend. He braked a little too sharply and swerved into the ditch, doing a great deal of damage to the Mercedes. A common enough occurrence, except that it happened just at the point where the old corpse path crossed the new motor road: the ditch he ended up in was part of the old road. And, which was more surprising, there was in fact no other car. Lance decided he must have seen the reflection of his own headlights, although a careful search revealed no reflective material at the place.

It was not until the last days of that summer that there was any further untoward incident that might be connected with the disturbance to the old track. Things had gone very much as Lance had foreseen: the few locals using the route had obligingly diverted around the side of the field; the Ramblers had made one organized sortie right across the middle on the line of the old path, damaging the young barley, but had not repeated their protest, and the plants had recovered. It looked like being a record yield: the land was in excellent heart, the weather kind. He would make £400 or £500 an acre: its value as pasture was less than half that. Say, £2,000 clear profit, and the chance to use some of that fine new machinery that was lying idle. To say nothing of the pheasants he had laid down – three hundred this year, as happy as sandboys in the growing corn, which would fatten handsomely on the leavings.

When the time came for harvesting there was some difficulty in manoeuvring the big machines into the field, the gates and approaches not having been designed for anything so large; but once started the operation went well enough. Most of the pheasants had been discouraged from staying in the corn, but one or two remained and from time to time rose with flurried shrieks of alarm right in front of the combine harvester.

Lance was walking round with a gun, accounting for any rabbits that might emerge, and keeping an eye on things generally. In spite of his disdain for superstition he could not avoid a shudder as the lumbering harvester crossed the path of the old road for the first time. As cut succeeded cut he perceived, much to his discomfort, that the track which he had thought to have destroyed emerged quite clearly: the corn there was a subtly different colour from that in the rest of the field. Probably, he thought, some chemical reaction, but nonetheless disturbing: he found himself returning to the old path many times during his walk round the field, as if to make sure that its resurrection was indeed a fact.

He was actually standing on the path when it happened. Although it was a fine warm day a sudden chill descended, as if a cloud had passed before the sun. It was very cold indeed, and he shivered. Something seemed to be moving in the corner of the field, where the old road emerged from the tunnel. The mouth of the tunnel was black in the bright sunlight, but he could swear that there was something moving in it. The blackness seemed to emerge like a dense vapour, streaming down the path towards him, mutating as it came into a host of indefinable shapes, gesturing, writhing and threatening, not thinning like smoke might as they drew away from the tunnel but seeming to gather force and solidity from the earth itself along the line of the path – and along that path, direct and inexorable, death approached him.

Lance had his gun, and the instincts of a shooter. He let off both barrels into the cloud, now only a few feet away: he could see the muzzle flash clearly against the foul vapour, but the implacable advance continued. He stepped back.

What happened thereafter was well described in the columns of the *Kirby Standale Telegraph and Argus*, published some weeks later.

The inquest into the tragic accident that took place on 16 August at Standale Grange was held in the Church Chambers on Wednesday afternoon.

Mr John Fenton, labourer, described how Mr Lancelot Wharton, tenant at Standale Grange, was supervising the harvesting of the barley crop in a field known as Hall Bottom. Mr Wharton had been shooting rabbits and was carrying a loaded gun at the time. According to Mr Fenton's testimony Mr Wharton raised his gun and fired apparently straight in front of him, although nothing was visible there. He then stepped backwards, as if to reload, and went right into the path of the oncoming combine harvester.

Mr George Turnbull, driving the harvester, affirmed that the whole thing happened so quickly there was no time to take any preventative action. Not only did the tractor pass over Mr Wharton's body, but further injuries were inflicted by the blades of the harvester. Mr Wharton was pronounced dead on arrival at the Royal Infirmary Carlisle.

Dr James McGillvray confirmed that Mr Wharton seemed to have been in good health, although the body had been so mutilated as to make accurate examination difficult.

A verdict of accidental death was returned, the coroner, Dr Farrer Metcalf, adding a rider that too much care could hardly be taken when dealing with the complex and dangerous machinery now so common in agricultural industry.

Readers may recall a long correspondence that took place last year on the subject of ploughing Hall Bottom, which had until that time been a permanent pasture containing botanical rarities. It is much to be regretted that the first crop there should have been attended by so shocking a fatality.

The mind has mountains

'You're off to France with Crumhorn, I hear?'

'Well, yes, I suppose I am,' replied Treadgold. 'Of course, I'd forgotten for a moment. He's in your line of business, isn't he?'

The Birtleian Professor of Neurology nodded. 'Hope you get on all right, that's all.'

Treadgold was ready for a little academic scandal, and correctly sensed something lying behind the Professor's remark: the Combination Room seemed an appropriate place in which to develop the story. 'Why, is he a difficult sort of character?'

'Not difficult, by any means. The fellow's charm itself. Talked himself nearly to the top of the tree. Still not forty, married twice, first wife died young, and left him quite a bit of money. Second got fed up rather quickly and left him. No, it's that he has rather an odd reputation in our branch of the trade.' An interrogative eyebrow from Treadgold was enough to ensure the Professor's continuing.

'Rather a heroic experimenter, you might say. But how did you two get together? He's not a member of our university, and there's not much in common between your medieval history and his neurology, is there? Not venturing into ultracrepidarianism, are you?'

'We met back at Cambridge at a Trinity Feast,' Treadgold explained, ignoring the ridiculous word for the moment, but resolving to look it up as soon as possible. 'You get all sorts there, and as it happened we were both undergraduates at about the same time. We happened to start talking about France, and he'd, rather flatteringly I thought, read my article in "History Today" on churches of the Saintonge. Just a piece on the Romanesque sculptures you find there. Only of popular interest, of course. I explained that I was planning another on the Quercy area, and since he was going to a university conference in Toulouse at almost exactly the same time, it looked like a good idea to travel together. Indeed he offered to help me with the photography. He seemed really quite well informed . . .' Treadgold was about to add 'for a scientist', but checked himself in time and went on, 'But what do you mean – a heroic experimenter?'

The Fellows in the University of Durham do not take their port from a communal board, as is the custom in the other two ancient Universities – Dunelmians do not acknowledge the godless institution in Gower Street as anything but an overblown polytechnic – but seated in a half-circle around the Combination Room fire, each with his own small wine table. The Professor shifted himself, table and chair, nearer to Treadgold and settled down for a confidential exposure of Crumhorn's sins.

'Crumhorn has something of a reputation in his own field, which is generally concerned with conditioned responses. Of course he's a young man in a hurry, and like many such takes a number of short cuts. Work not always entirely validated: generalizations without considering possible objections. But that's by no means unusual. No, Crumhorn's trouble is rather more serious.' The butler came round, and provided a dramatic pause. 'Thank you, I'll stay with the hock.' The Professor continued, 'He works a lot with animals, as you might imagine. Now, in spite of everything the anti-vivisectionists say, animal experiments are usually very strictly controlled. Even if scientists are sometimes tempted to cut corners, the laboratory technicians would never let them.'

'But Crumhorn cuts corners?'

'Nearly had his license revoked, which would have been almost unheard of. Some of the things he got away with were by any standards very nasty. And since then he's lain low, official-ly. We are all pretty sure he's been getting animals from unauthorized sources – he has that private money and a quite well-equipped lab at his home, I believe – and putting them through it. His publications keep coming out, and that's the main thing for scientists, you know. Any suggestion that he might be misusing experimental animals would be treated by him as professional jealousy, and we wouldn't like that. It's not just mice, either; his work needs access to a whole range of animals – cats, dogs, monkeys, and goodness knows what besides. I'd rather not think about what happens to them.'

Treadgold was alarmed. 'Why, you make him sound like a second Dr Moreau. He seemed inoffensive enough to me. Do you think it would be better to call off the expedition?'

The Professor smiled, and sipped his hock.

'Oh, I don't think he'll start slicing bits off you, old fellow. Now, if you were an Alsatian, say, you'd have cause for concern.' The Professor laughed moderately at his own joke. 'You'll find him an agreeable enough travelling companion, I'm sure. Yes, thank you, I will try a cigar.'

And indeed the expedition promised well. Treadgold left early on the day of departure to meet Crumhorn, who had been visiting the University of Sussex, on the boat at Newhaven. They had both agreed that Dieppe was much the pleasantest of the channel ports, and the drive from there, over the Pont de Tancarville and down to the Loire, much the most agreeable way of travelling south.

Treadgold was somewhat surprised at Crumhorn's appear-ance. On their previous meeting he had been in decent subfusc, but in holiday mood he was another man, positively fashionable in a roll-neck sweater and cardigan, a gold bracelet and those ubiquitous athletic shoes affected by the sedentary as daily wear. Perhaps this could be taken as typical of the University of Newcastle, where Crumhorn had his Readership? Treadgold was a hairy tweed coat, corduroy trousers and brown brogues man himself. And the camera equipment Crumhorn carried was extensive beyond Treadgold's experience.

'I have to do a lot of this with my work,' Crumhorn explained. 'Photographic records are very important: and I've done a bit of architectural work before. You need a few lenses, and it's useful to have a couple of bodies loaded with different film, since the light changes are so marked.'

Crumhorn proved everything that could be expected of a travelling companion, considerate and courteous but not over talkative, navigating, once they had disembarked, with precision, and driving, when it was his turn, with reassuring competence.

The outlines of their journey were agreed: they were to spend the first night at the Hotel Dauphin at L'Aigle, where a room had been booked, and then to take the autoroute from Tours straight to their first stop at Moissac, some fifty kilometres from Toulouse, travelling thence to Souillac and ending up in Toulouse itself where they would go their separate ways, Crumhorn to his conference, Treadgold to seek out a correspondent in the Musée des Augustins who, he hoped, might put him on the track of some less well-known churches in the area.

The Hotel Dauphin, which has had one rosette in Michelin for many years, provided an excellent dinner (the kidneys are especially recommended) in the old style, having no truck with the raspberry vinegar, raw fish and small helpings of the *nouvelle cuisine*. The rich food and wine proved, as they so often do, a stimulus to that weighty but vague philosophical conversation which satisfies most agreeably at the time, but whose content, when an endeavour is made later to call it to mind, proves so elusive.

The name of the town led inevitably to a discussion of the Emperor Napoleon. Treadgold advanced the view held by all historians, except among the unregenerate and chauvinistic French, that Napoleon was the direct cause of untold misery, death, and suffering and should be ranked with Genghis Khan, St Bernard, Hitler and Stalin as monstrous enemies of mankind. He went further, carried away by the Calvados, and pointed out that only those countries who had resisted the French Revolution and clung to their monarchies had any claim now to be called democratic and settled. How infinitely better off the Russians would be now under the Romanovs, constitutionalized by Kerensky and with an infusion of sensible middle-class blood, than under their current chaotic and barbaric despotism! How much preferable was Queen Elizabeth as a Head of State than President X or Y!

While Crumhorn had to admit the force of these arguments he defended the Emperor warmly as a protector of the diffusion of knowledge and the advancement of science: he listed the achievements of French savants in the early nineteenth century and the tradition of investigative scholarship that had then been established. He seemed to have a personal devotion to Napoleon that sounded to Treadgold a little unhealthy. Napoleon, he said, was a man of destiny who took great decisions and generated events of shattering importance. If misery resulted, this was unavoidable; the world could not be changed, as changed it most certainly must be, without suffering. Pain and death were as natural as birth, and inevitable concomitants to the progress of mankind.

Since neither man was listening too closely to what the other said, each being occupied with polishing his own arguments, both ended up well enough pleased with their discussion. It was only later, in very different circumstances, that Treadgold recalled some of the more disquieting aspects of Crumhorn's philosophy.

They were up next morning in good time, only a little liverish, and had an uneventful journey of some 800 kilometres to Moissac, where they arrived at the hour of the aperitif, too late for work but in good time to find a room in the Hotel Chapon Fin just around the corner from the church. Being experienced travellers they had agreed, for reasons of economy, to share a room, knowing that this would by no means cause eyebrows to be raised as they might have been in England.

Before dinner they inspected the outside of the church: an advantage of Moissac is that the great feature, the south door, is available for inspection at any time, being on the exterior of the building. It is, if you do not happen to know it, a remarkable piece of Romanesque art. In England the only Romanesque style is the Norman which, in its craggy and ponderous austerity seen at its most perfect in Treadgold's university cathedral, is far removed from the intensely lively and active work of Southern French artists who inherited a Roman tradition with an altogether sprightlier feel to it. As much as the friezes of fifth-century Greece – or possibly even more – the art of twelfth-century Languedoc gives an impression of vivid, even violent, animation.

The tympanum at Moissac shows the vision of St John the Evangelist, literally petrified for eight centuries but every bit as commanding and striking as when the first stone was hewn. The double door is framed with huge serrations, for all the world like the jaws of some monstrous creature from the past. At either side of the door the reveals are ornamented with various scenes: those on the east have rather jolly accounts of the Annunciation, Adoration and Presentation; on the west there are two large panels representing the sins of avarice and lechery – the latter depicting, most unusually, a naked woman with two snakes attached to her breasts and some nameless beasts to her private parts, presumably (though not very obviously) attacking her. Both men stood silent for some moments, overwhelmed by the vigour of the work, before Crumhorn was moved, in spite of the poor light, to try some shots with a 1000 ASA film, which he felt might produce an interesting effect when enlarged.

Dinner that night was not as rich as that which they had enjoyed previously, a fact which they welcomed rather than otherwise, but which did not lead to the same deep conversation. They chatted instead, listening more carefully than before, about their different occupations. Treadgold complained of the great wealth of historical evidence that remained to be collated before any firm judgements could be made, and of how research had to be concentrated on points of specialized interest that were nevertheless the only acceptable methods of arriving at a general theory that might become acceptable.

For his part Crumhorn described the frustrations of the scientific enquirer, the many theories to be examined, and the obstacles that were put in his path: not obstacles of technique, for those were inevitable, but artificial barriers of committees to be satisfied, rules to be obeyed, obstructive regulations to be circumvented. 'If it wasn't for all the complacent mediocrities whose only concern is to ensure that none of the younger men ever get anything done, we could move forward with huge strides. Have you thought how much could be done with just a little sensible genetic engineering? How much human knowledge might be advanced if we knew more about learning-patterns? But what do you get? Bumbling interference at every turn!

'Take the inheritance of acquired behaviour. It seems clear that mice can transmit information they have been taught to their offspring, even if they have no physical contact with them, by some sort of programming. The young mice are born with the knowledge that their parents have gained. And there's a man in Australia who has produced some evidence that rats can transmit acquired behaviour to other rats in a quite different part of the world.'

'Almost as if the Great Rat in the sky handed things down,' murmured Treadgold. His frivolity was ignored.

'But we must have evidence, and it's damned hard to get. Cats and dogs are much more useful to work with, but it's impossible to get anywhere with all the fuddy-duddy regulations we have to cope with.' For an instant the light of fanaticism shone in Crumhorn's eyes, and the historian began, somewhat anxiously, to recall what he had heard of his reputation. The moment passed, however, and the rest of the evening elapsed without any other exhibition of enthusiasm – using the word in its old pejorative sense – excepting the marked approbation with which he greeted the really excellent *tarte aux mirabelles*. Treadgold was conscious however, that his room-mate passed a less peaceful night than previously, tossing and turning a good deal.

The morning saw them at work in the early sun. There was much to photograph – the great doorway itself, the massive capitals of the tower, and the immense collection in the cloister – seventy-six capitals of Old Testament scenes, each with its angels, prophets, beasts and monsters.

Treadgold greatly admired the professionalism with which Crumhorn set about his task, plotting a series of angles to suit the light, arranging his equipment, which seemed to be the most expensive and varied possible, and working ceaselessly. In all Crumhorn must have taken more than two hundred pictures, and Treadgold became a little concerned about the expense. Crumhorn was dismissive. 'Film's cheap enough, and we need only print the ones you want to use. I've got a little chap who'll do that for a song. One's got to be careful about whom one lets see what, and he's discreet as well as cheap. He produces some very decent results. And if I can have one or two of the best, I'll be very happy: it's just the sort of thing I love doing.'

Only one peculiar incident occurred during a busy and productive day. Crumhorn was greatly struck by the capitals in the tower, especially one depicting wolves carrying off geese, and another with lions tearing at each other. Their situation made photography without artificial lighting difficult, and Crumhorn had to enlist Treadgold's help in placing flashes which, he explained, he normally avoided like the plague.

'But we must have that wolf, old boy. Look at his eyes – wicked, aren't they? – defiant, cruel even. Unbelievable what those fellows could do with a lump of stone.'

The work finished, they set off tired but well satisfied for the second church at Souillac, some ninety minutes' drive away.

The fame of the town of Souillac has always depended on its abbey, and since the abbey was pretty thoroughly destroyed in the Wars of Religion, the fame of the abbey itself rests on a solitary artefact: the remains of another portal. Although damaged – one support is entirely missing – it is perhaps even more impressive than the famous Moissac door.

The tympanum, which usually in these parts depicts Christ in Majesty, the Last Judgement, or the Revelation, at Souillac surprisingly and uniquely describes the interesting legend of Theophilus. This monk, the principal financial officer of the abbey, was deposed of his honorable and lucrative post by the intrigues of his fellow monks. In order to regain his influence he made a pact with a demon to sell his soul in exchange for his restored office. Naturally enough he repented of this, and the Virgin Mary appeared to him in a dream to restore his phylactery (the badge of office) to him. If Theophilus is not already the patron saint of the unemployed, he ought to be.

Although the demon is quite realistically – if that is not too improper a word – rendered, the whole is a pleasant and innocuous piece of work.

The surviving column is a very different kettle of fish. To begin with, it should be explained that the word 'column', with its connotations of classical orders, is misleading. The support of the Souillac tympanum is a vertical chaos of writhing, screaming and agonizing human and animal life. The face of the support is composed of interlaced birds and animals – eagles, lions, griffins, wolves, all snatching and clawing at each other. The left-hand reveal depicts contorted human figures clutching and tearing wildly at each other, struggling and falling headlong, expressing the utmost pangs of fear and pain. The whole is, one supposes, an analogy of the torments of hell which Theophilus managed to avoid.

Following the repeated and destructive pillaging of the abbey during the wars, the sole remaining treasure, the portal, was protected by being rebuilt inside, as the west door leading from the nave to the pro-nave. By the time Treadgold and Crumhorn arrived, the whole church had been locked for the night and an examination of the portal was therefore impossible.

In any event they would have had little time at their disposal since Treadgold had previously arranged to dine that night with Maître Paul Desnoyer, the retired lawyer from Toulouse with whom he had previously been in correspondence, and who had something of a reputation as an expert on the Romanesque churches of the region. M. Desnoyer turned out, when they met for dinner at their hotel, Les Granges Vielles, a little way out of the town, to be both well informed and helpful. He had made a special study of the Moissac cloister, and had identified all the hundreds of personages carved on the capitals, a task of some complexity. These results he was happy to put at the disposal of Mr Treadgold: they had previously been published in the *Journal des Etudes Occitanes*, and he would be delighted to witness their wider diffusion in the English press. In return he would be happy to receive some copies of the doubtless excellent work being carried out.

French being the weakest of his languages, Dr Crumhorn played only a minor part in this discussion; but he did justice to the cassoulet they all shared. After the cheese Crumhorn began to question Maître Desnoyer on the background to the Moissac sculptures, which had clearly left a deep impression on him.

'They are a pretty savage lot, and when you think they were originally all coloured, the whole array must have looked horrific. Not the sort of thing you expect to see in a church.'

'You should appreciate,' the lawyer explained, 'that even in the Age of Faith the church was an extremely practical institution. Churchmen lived on gifts given both by princes and barons, but also, willingly or unwillingly, by the peasants and bourgeois. The church was for them a theatre, a spectacle, a consulting room, the centre and focus of their lives: but they often liked to get away without paying for their pleasure. So, since ticket offices and cashiers hadn't been invented, they made sure that people were put in the right frame of mind before going into a church. They should be reminded of the Glory of God, the pains of Hell fire – and Hell fire especially for the mean, by which they understood those who hadn't given generously to Mother Church.

'There is in Toulouse a most striking example: the west front of the Augustines' church is entirely built of plain brick, a massive structure quite bare of ornament except for one stone carved over the door. It shows a man in agony being torn apart by a great hound and an eagle, but clutching desperately at his purse, the filling of which had been his only goal in life. And at Moissac you will remember the same thing, but nearly life-sized, next to the adulteress and the serpents. Oh yes, they made most certain that purse-strings would be loose on entering a church – and recollect that at this time there was a fixed tariff – so many years' remission of purgatory for a sou, hundreds of thousands for a gold piece, pardons for specific sins – a sort of spiritual supermarket.'

The Englishmen appreciated the explanation. 'It's queer, isn't it though?' observed Treadgold. 'They used animals to torment people, rather than demons or devils, say.'

'Merely orthodox, dear sir.' The Maître was delighted to have the opportunity of enlightening a distinguished professional. 'You doubtless recall that witches and demons, although they exist in the Bible, are not there to torment the damned. The creatures of Hell are tempters rather than instruments of punishment, and the earlier Middle Ages found it easier to think in terms of animals, sometimes fabulous but mostly usually real, visiting retribution upon the evildoer. Perhaps they thought it only reasonable that animals, having suffered at the hands of men should, as you say, "get their own back?"'

Maître Desnoyer was pleased at his successful use of an English idiom – one received respectfully, at least by Tread-gold. Crumhorn was not sympathetic. 'What a ridiculous set of ideas. Those people may have been our ancestors, but their whole way of life was so different they're almost like an alien race. Look at their intellectual horizon: they didn't have a clue about any scientific process; they'd lost all that the Greeks had learned; and they refused to learn anything from the Arabs, who took things like that seriously. Everything in the world about them was a fog of superstition and myth. No wonder they depended on a lot of spiritual mumbo-jumbo to give them any sort of guidance. Really, when you think of it, that's why their works of art are so interesting; they were wonderful artists, but worked in a cloud of ignorance.'

Treadgold resisted the temptation to riposte with Richard Rolle, and the conversation petered out when the sorbet succeeded the cheese. M. Desnoyer drove back to his home in Toulouse, leaving the Englishmen to a relatively early night.

Treadgold was woken in the night by the smell of cigarette smoke. He was annoyed. Not only did he disapprove of smoking at any time, but in one's bedroom it really was too much. Pushing the covers from his head he was immediately aware that the light was on. Crumhorn was sitting up in bed staring at the pages of a book and puffing away at a revolting French cigarette. 'Is there anything the matter?' asked Treadgold.

'No, no, I just couldn't sleep that's all. Must be the cassoulet, rather rich for me perhaps,' said Crumhorn, carelessly.

Treadgold lay for a while studying Crumhorn and wondering what to say about the cigarette. Admittedly there was only one more night to be shared with his companion, but really he could not bear the thought of continued smoking. He coughed affectedly, but this produced no result. Finally he said, 'I think perhaps tomorrow night we might have separate rooms. I find it difficult to sleep with, with, er, that cigarette.'

'Oh, I am sorry, I'll stop at once,' said Crumhorn, and extinguished his cigarette. 'There is no need to go to such expense . . . I really don't need to smoke, it's just habit, I suppose.'

Content for the moment with this reply, Treadgold, being fully awake, decided to take advantage of the moment. He put on his dressing-gown, and thanking Crumhorn for his consideration, made for the door. His action seemed to disturb his companion, who asked, rather sharply, 'Where are you off to?'

'Merely obeying a call of nature.'

'You won't be long – I mean, how silly of me, you are not feeling ill?'

'Not at all,' replied Treadgold and hastened from the room. Crumhorn did not sound at all himself: in fact he was being distinctly neurotic.

On returning to their room, Treadgold found the light still on and Crumhorn still reading. Although he himself was able to go back to sleep, dropping off speedily and remaining comatose until morning, he was half woken several times by Crumhorn stirring about in his bed, and even at times muttering inarticulately: once he gave a violent start and exclaimed, 'God!' so forcefully that Treadgold was momentarily alarmed. He resolved that the first thing he would do next day would be to go to a chemist and buy some cottonwool so that he could plug his ears and get a reasonable sleep the next night.

Nothing was said at breakfast, and the two men buckled down to the task of photographing the Souillac portal. This was to be their last project together since Crumhorn had to present himself at his conference on the following day.

It proved trickier than their earlier work. The doorway being inside a rather gloomy church, there was no possibility of much being done without quite extensive artificial lighting, which involved obtaining permission to do so, hiring equipment, and finding a suitable power supply. As Treadgold's French was considerably the more fluent, most of the work fell to him, but in spite of his best efforts it was midday before the arrangements had been made for the equipment to be delivered – after luncheon, naturally, all activity being suspended during that sacred period.

As though this delay was not enough, Treadgold was annoyingly accosted by an old man as he was about to enter the church on his return from finalizing his preparations. The old fellow seemed, by his dress, to be some sort of verger, but his accent was so thick, and his speech so impeded by some badly fitting dentures as to make him almost incomprehensible. Treadgold understood him to advance some sort of warning against photographing the sculptures – they were unlucky . . . beasts of the past, but not of the past . . . a bad time of year . . . evil stirring . . . humanity frail . . . revenge . . . Imprecise but disturbing, especially on an empty stomach.

Treadgold assured the old man, speaking slowly and distinctly in his best French, that they intended no harm, were most grateful for his kind advice, and would be sure to tidy up after they had finished. He was rewarded by a blank stare of incomprehension, but the old man shuffled off. It was strange, but Treadgold was sure he saw him cross himself as he went.

In spite of this adventitious aid they had their work cut out. The cables were not long enough to reach the places Crumhorn considered necessary, and had to be joined: a trestle and a pair of steps had to be pressed into service; two bulbs failed and replacements had to be sought. By the time all was done both men were exhausted. 'You see what I mean about artificial lighting,' grumbled Crumhorn, 'more bother than it's worth. Probably look awful too. Anyway, it's a beastly bit of work, at that.'

Nothing Treadgold could suggest produced any improvement in Crumhorn's spirits. He had developed a headache, was feeling liverish, a glass of Evian was all he could stomach: but rather than taking a little Macleans stomach powder and going to bed early, he stayed toying with his food and talking disjointedly while Treadgold ate steadily through his own dinner.

Crumhorn, when the meal was finished, insisted on accompanying Treadgold on a stroll around the country lanes surrounding the hotel, which were well illuminated by a brilliant full moon, and then tried to persuade him to go into a rather seedy bar for a night-cap. Treadgold preferred to return to the hotel, pointing out that both of them had had a disturbed night and needed to be up early in the morning.

On returning to the hotel they saw the lethargic guard-dog, too well fed to do anything other than stretch out at the foot of the stairs. It was a comforting sight. Any burglar would have to step over the animal, and in the dark would not know how gentle a creature it was. But as Treadgold carefully stepped over it, it rose, laid back its ears and snarled at Crumhorn. Crumhorn stopped, visibly shaken, and then pulling himself together exclaimed, 'Dreadful animal,' and hurried up the stairs after Treadgold.

When Treadgold returned from the bathroom he found Crumhorn to all outward signs peacefully asleep, but with his bedside light still on. Treadgold decided not to switch it off, but rolled some cottonwool ear-plugs, placed them gently in his ears, wrapped a silk handkerchief round his eyes, and lay down, determined that nothing would disturb his night's slumber.

But it was his turn to be wakeful. Foolishly, perhaps, he had eaten both the *gratin de langoustines* and the preserved goose, and these took their effect. On rising at about four in the morning, he noticed that Crumhorn's bed was empty. It could be, of course, that his companion had gone out of the room to smoke a cigarette, but Treadgold was sufficiently worried to lie awake. It was not until six, with still no sign of Crumhorn, that he thought to look for his friend's clothes. Certainly those that he had worn the previous day seemed to be there, and, as far as he could see, so was the rest of his wardrobe. Now seriously worried, Treadgold hurriedly dressed and set off to make enquiries.

The staff were already stirring but they had neither heard nor seen anything of the gentleman. It was a mild summer night, but even an Englishman would hardly have gone for a walk in his pyjamas. After making a few casts about the vicinity Treadgold felt that he ought to alert the police, and made his way to the station. The *brigadier* on duty was clearly worried and muttered something about its being unhealthy to be about at night under a full moon, especially at that time of year. He would send out some men immediately.

The country round Souillac is hilly and well wooded, a difficult place for searchers, so Treadgold knew he might have to wait for several hours before news came. Feeling that coffee and fresh croissants would be soothing he collected a newspaper and returned to the hotel to await events. He could not explain to himself the reason for his growing agitation. Crumhorn was, after all quite capable of looking after himself. It could well be that he had dressed and gone out for a walk, putting on top of his pyjamas clothes which Treadgold had not seen before. With these thoughts in mind he was better able to enjoy his breakfast, and read *Le Monde* from cover to cover, even trying his hand at the crossword.

The hours passed, and when finally news came it was not good.

'Would Mr Treadgold please give himself the trouble to visit the *mairie*?' A car was waiting. The *maire* was with the commandant of police. The searchers had found a trail, and the dogs had been able to follow it for some kilometres into the depths of the wood. It seemed that the gentleman had not paid too much attention to where he was going, and had apparently moved at a great pace, leaving torn scraps of his clothing on various thorns and branches. He was found to be safe, it was true, but much distressed, and had evinced striking emotion at the appearance of the police dogs.

They presented Treadgold with a bedraggled Crumhorn wrapped in a blanket, shivering and delirious, with the concierge trying to make him take a little brandy. It was obvious that he had to be got home at once.

Treadgold surprised himself by remaining remarkably cool: he coped with the consul, the telephoning, and arranging a private plane to fly Crumhorn back; he cut short his own plans and, with conscious virtue, saw the unfortunate scientist safely into the arms of the National Health Service at Newcastle Airport.

Physically Crumhorn recovered quickly, but his mental equilibrium had been badly disturbed and he was sent to 'convalesce' in a hospital specializing in nervous disorders. Since this was not too far away, Treadgold felt it only civil to visit him there. The first of these visits took place just before the beginning of term, about two weeks after the Souillac incident.

He found Crumhorn fit enough and calm, although he suspected this to be the result of sedation. 'I'm terribly sorry to have been so much trouble, old chap. I can't think what went wrong. They say it was overwork, but damn it, I was on holiday. I believe it was all physical – some bug that affects the nervous system – plenty of them about, especially in such a rotten unhygienic place.' Treadgold thought this rather ungracious, but murmured polite agreement.

His next visit was to be the last. Crumhorn was ready to be discharged and seemed his old ebullient self. They exchanged affable trivialities, and Treadgold returned to his work relieved that a worrying episode had been satisfactorily terminated.

The term passed and the two men kept in touch, but only just. It was February before they met again, as a result of a rather agitated telephone call from Crumhorn. 'Look, can you possibly get over to Newcastle rather quickly? There is something I must talk about, and you're the only one who might understand.'

The long-suffering Treadgold did as he was bidden (after all Crumhorn's photography had been a tremendous success, and his publisher had hinted at an advance, a most uncharacteristic notion) and presented himself at Crumhorn's fine old Victorian house in Jesmond. The interior had been gutted, presumably when the laboratory was installed, and Treadgold was led into a bright, even glossy, sitting-room with Scandinavian furniture, hand-woven rugs, and a collection of lights giving the illumination level of a television studio.

By contrast Crumhorn was grey and agitated, holding himself on the tightest of reins, his hands exploring each other as he spoke in a search for a reassurance that was not forthcoming. He did his duty as a host, and provided them both with substantial whiskies.

'It is good of you to come, but I've got to try to explain things, and you're the only person who might understand. You see, it

164

all started when we were in France. Do you remember that night when we were talking about genetic transmission of learned behaviour – the rats inheriting information? You talked about the Great Rat in the sky? God, what a complacent idiot I was!'

Crumhorn stopped and looked at his hands, holding them motionless for a moment.

'All those sculptures were about rewards and punishment, especially punishment. I'm a scientist, and I believe in the logical assessment of evidence. And that brings some pretty frightening hypotheses forward. Don't go thinking I'm dotty, by the way – my work is still as good as ever it was. But that just makes it all the more terrifying. Lots of people break up, imagine things – quite normal, if unpleasant. I'm not seeing strange pursuers in the shadows, you understand. It doesn't seem necessary to assume demons or werewolves as agents of retribution. Men generally contrive to be their own judges and executioners.'

He stared again at his hands, and looked up with a faint smile, the old Crumhorn reasserting itself.

'That's it, old boy. Thank you for turning up and being patient. Let me freshen your drink. I just wanted you to understand, when it happens.'

There was not a great deal Treadgold could do, other than express a comprehension he did not truly possess even although he continued to puzzle over the matter for some days after.

He did not have to wait too long for the next and final development. A telephone call came from the local police: could he make it convenient to see an officer from the North-umberland force that afternoon? It was really quite important.

He could, and was duly visited by a polite and tactful inspector. 'I'm sorry to tell you, sir, that your friend Dr Crumhorn has met with an accident. Yes, I'm afraid he's dead. Of course we know that he had been under treatment for sometime, so it was not unexpected, but the hospital told us that he talked a good deal about you, and we hoped that you might be able to tell us something about his recent state of mind.'

Treadgold did not feel up to explaining what he thought Crumhorn might have meant at their last meeting; that would have taken far too long and been of little help. But he confirmed that Crumhorn had expressed feelings of anxiety and depression, and ventured to enquire what exactly had happened.

'Well, sir, it seems that he decided to go for a drive in the middle of the night – and that must have been two nights back. He'd gone on the A66 and got just past Bowes when he ran out of petrol. It's pretty bleak and unpleasant on Stainmore, but he seems to have left the car and struck out across the moor. He'd got some way, four or five miles, and at quite a pace, up towards one of those old Roman forts, or signal stations, I suppose they were. Almost as though he was running away from something.

'There's a lot of limestone pavement around there – outcrops of rock with crevasses and holes of all shapes. The Durham lads found him wedged tight in one of the crevasses – he must have pushed himself in quite hard – just as though he was trying to hide.'

'And he'd died of exposure?' Treadgold asked, rather anxiously.

The inspector looked somewhat embarrassed. 'I'd hoped not to have gone into it, since it's not too pleasant, but the body when we discovered it was badly mutilated. It was a couple of days before we found him, and the lower half of the body, outside the crevasse, had been scattered.'

'But how on earth . . .?' asked the horrified Treadgold.

'Oh, your friend died from natural causes, as they say, but after that, well – foxes, I'm afraid. They live in the pavements, you know. It's happened before that someone has died of exposure, and if the body isn't found soon enough it makes an easy meal for a growing family of cubs. Only thing that struck me though was that, judging from the marks, it must have been a real big old vixen.'

166

The familiar

When Dr Myles Myddleton had occasion to travel north from King's Cross Station he found the journey usually to be both pleasant and relaxing. To an architectural historian, Cubitt's spare and elegant terminus, marred though it is by a British Rail glass and plastic ticket office, could not be other than invigorating, a foretaste of the clear skies and clean lines of the North. Then other architectural and topological treats were to be savoured: Hinchingbrooke glimpsed through trees, Peterborough rising above the fens; the stately spires of Grantham and Newark; the golden Minster at York; and the crowning glory of Durham soaring up across the valley of the Wear. If one continued, there were still to come the striking view of the Tyne, its north bank crowned by castle and churches, the stark and sandy splendour of the Tweed with Bamburgh and Lindisfarne standing on the Eastern March, and the final dramatic seascapes from the Border to Musselburgh. And, considering more mundane matters, the service, timekeeping and food on the Eastern Region were consistently better than that on the old LMS line from Euston.

But in spite of these expected delights, aesthetic and fleshly, Dr Myddleton – his was a doctorate of philosophy, the usage of which in social life is so much to be deplored, although Myddleton did so whenever possible, a fact that tells us something of the man – was not happy as he boarded the Flying Scotsman that Tuesday morning.

The cause was obvious enough: the night before had been succeeded by the morning after. It had started when he had agreed to meet his old friend and colleague Maximus Drysdale in the bar of the Architectural Association. While Myddleton established himself as an art historian, his contemporary Drysdale had become a practising architect, if that description does not convey too much the idea of one closely concerned with the actual construction of buildings. Drysdale was well known for his exciting new projects, which often won prizes in international competitions but which were never, for some reason, translated into solider terms. The resulting paucity of fees had forced Maximus to take a teaching post with the Architectural Association in order to supply his daily needs.

Myddleton had been, he now admitted to himself, tactless. After a couple of gins in the bar the two men had walked around the current exhibition. It was unfortunate that this had consisted almost entirely of rather beautiful drawings of extensive and magnificent buildings. No mundane plans or photographs were to be seen and reference to the catalogue, an expensive and handsomely presented affair, confirmed that the architect being honoured had in his entire professional career actually supervised only one bricks-and-mortar job, the conversion of a flat for his brother.

This information, together with the fragments of conversation that floated earnestly around – 'intensity of spatial awareness . . . revolutionary concept of static dynamics . . . creative tension . . . socially acceptable predication . . .' – falling from the lips of lithe and seemly blondes and bald, bearded gentlemen of portly habits of body drove Myddleton into a spasm of indignation. He was, although not without his own pretensions, an enthusiast for honest craftsmanship and the skills of the master builder.

'Christ, Max, what a collection of phoneys! Can you ever let them loose? I'd love to see them chatting to an Irish foreman. Don't this lot ever build anything nowadays?'

Considering the sparseness of Maximus's own output – an elegant gazebo, a couple of modest houses, and joint work on a health centre or so – this was undiplomatic, and set the tone for a sour evening. Argument had continued over a curry, a form of nourishment calling for an untroubled digestion. Hard things said over the onion bhajis: Maximus had pointed out that he at least was addressing himself to the problems of the day, not 'dusting off old houses that were idle museums or the last refuges of a decadent artistocracy'; that 'it was the ludicrous distortion of priorities in a consumerist society that restricted the opportunities for architects'; and that the readers of *Country Life*, the outlet for much of Myddleton's work, were mainly to blame for this sorry state of things.

Myddleton had fought back through the vindaloo – a mistake, that dish – and ended up at the jellabi stage with some remarks on the subject of middle-aged queers that would have been much better left unsaid. They had parted with mutual expressions of disesteem.

After that unpromising evening his night had been disastrous: an hour or two of sleep interspersed with acute gastric discomfort, giving way at dawn to a slumber from which he had been prematurely awakened to catch his train. He had a nasty headache and no appetite for breakfast.

Given time, however, the train journey exercised its own therapy: when Selby swung into view, elegant and white, Myles felt well enough to accept a cup of coffee from the attendant, and after Newcastle made a sally to the buffet car for a bacon sandwich, a pork pie, and two cans of Newcastle brown ale: he was not, you might gather, altogether sound on dietary principles, and this had done much to ensure a comfortable roundness of contour that made for difficulties in some aspects of his work, such as negotiating scaffolding or exploring ice-houses.

At thirty-nine Myddleton had already done much; he had developed a considerable, even an international, reputation as an architectural historian and written a number of clear, popular and accurate books, intelligently illustrated, which had sold well and illuminated some obscure corners of the subject. His best known work was *The Other Adam* a *catalogue raisonné* of the work of James Adam, brother of the better-known Robert. Scottish architects of the seventeenth and eighteenth centuries were indeed his speciality: he allowed himself to go as far towards the present day as Playfair, who had at least been born in the eighteenth century, while his survey of the seventeenth century in Scotland, *The Pre-Adamites*, was regarded as the definitive work on that subject.

The books often had their genesis in surveys of individual houses written for that distinguished periodical of reference, *Country Life*, and it was such a commission that had brought him on his present journey, the purpose of which was to prepare an article on Peddie Abbey in Roxburghshire, one of the few houses built by James Adam alone. At least, this was Myddleton's contention: the attribution to James Adam was not universally accepted, and he was anxious to prove the truth of his thesis. To help in doing this he had enlisted the services of a local historian, one James Gillespie, a retired schoolmaster.

When Myddleton left the train at Dunbar, Gillespie was there to meet him. He was a man in his early sixties, active and capable, who proved to be enthusiastic and well informed on the matter in hand, but reserved and cautious on more general topics. The conversation in the car therefore plunged straight into the subject of Peddie Abbey.

'I know little of the architectural side, you understand, Dr Myddleton, but the written evidence I have should prove helpful. I was fortunate, very fortunate indeed, in securing much of the library of Peddie when the family sold out. I've sorted out those items that might possibly be useful to you and put them in the library up at the house: it'll be more convenient for you like that. There's not too much space back at the School House, where I stay.'

'That would be the sale before the Abbey was turned into a school, I suppose.'

'Aye, it was a big change. You'll find none of the original furniture, I fear, but the fabric of the house has been well cared for. Mind, you're fortunate not to be visiting in term time. A hundred and fifty wee girls would get in the way a bit.'

Myddleton paled at the thought: apart from one or two good

friends he was not keen on women at all, of any age, and the thought of so many shrill and unpredictable beings was frankly horrific.

As might be gathered from the numbers it was capable of accommodating, Peddie was a substantial house. Set among fine timber it commanded an extensive view over the Whiteadder valley: it was a three-storied edifice of nine bays with flanking wings. The *piano nobile*, an unusual feature in Scotland, was lofty, and illuminated by great Venetian windows in the central and terminal bays. There was no trace of any previous work, although there had been a substantial house on the site before the existing building: all that could now be seen was most purely classical. 'Of course it's Adam, and very fine Adam at that,' Myddleton thought to himself as they turned into the entrance court.

They were met – welcomed is altogether too enthusiastic a word for their reception – by Mrs Margulies, the domestic bursar, a lady accustomed to the exercise of authority.

'I've given you the visitors' room, Dr Myddleton, and you can use the library for your papers, but I must make it clear that all the staff are on holiday. There's no one in the house at all, for the servants live in the village and I will be here only in the afternoons. I have, however, arranged for Jennie Welsh, one of the kitchenmaids, to give you breakfast and leave you some cold meat and cheese for your supper. And you'll not be here but for the two days, I'm given to understand?'

Dr Myddleton was sufficiently annoyed by this to assert himself. 'I can't be too sure of that: it will all depend on how we get on. The proprietors are anxious, I believe, to have a full description made, and I always like to do things thoroughly. I will certainly let you know if I intend to remain longer.'

Mrs Margulies bristled, but then subsided, and the two men made off with some relief to the library, an elegant chamber although now with sadly empty shelves, to start work on documentation. Gillespie had not exaggerated, for his collection was extensive, one of the best records of country-house life that Myddleton had seen. Game books, stewards' accounts, wage books, visitors' books, kitchen and buttery books, factors' reports – all the records of the house were there, excepting the personal papers of the family, and, unfortunately for Myddleton, the builders' accounts. These, had they been available, would have formed clear proof of the name of the architect; as it was, he would have to be content with the solid testimony of the stone, which was already encouraging.

Gillespie, after explaining the sequence of the books, and pointing out some discoveries of which he was particularly proud, left Myddleton to his own devices, promising to return in the morning to assist with the survey. This arrangement suited Myles well enough, for he was able to take several pages of notes from the schoolmaster's material which would stand him in good stead not only for the commissioned article, but as material for a book on Scottish life and manners which he was planning.

After some hours' brisk work he was ready to sample Jennie's cold meat, which he found deplorable, accompanied as it was by bottled salad cream, wrapped sliced bread and plastic-covered cheese. He had, however, taken the precaution of bringing a bottle of whisky and so was able to supplement the sparse fare.

There was enough light remaining after this unsatisfactory meal to make possible a circuit of the exterior, so Myddleton set out to do this. The main house was spare, elegant and magnificent in the warm sunset glow; the unpolluted atmosphere had kept the hard outlines of the limestone unblurred, and the whole seemed a perfect epitome of the classical style. 'Of course, it's Adam, any idiot can see that,' Myddleton muttered triumphantly.

The stables were less impressive, having been taken over for storage and the elevations tampered with, although the tower and clock seemed to have remained intact. There was, he knew, the remains of a chapel somewhere nearby, over on the east side, a relic of Peddie's former abbatial status and therefore outside his period, but probably worth a look. It would be interesting to see whether it had been treated as a Gothick ruin, or merely left to moulder.

Access to the chapel proved difficult, through an overgrown and neglected shrubbery, but once reached the ruins proved to be all the most romantic could desire.

The building must have originally been on the most majestic scale – a church rather than an edifice intended for domestic devotions, and was, as could be seen from the remains, a work of the fourteenth century. The whole of the nave had been levelled, only the bases of the piers and moss-covered slabs indicating its dimensions, but the chancel, the whole of the north transept and a good proportion of the south had been preserved. Overgrown with creepers, shadowed by enormous elms which kept any vestige of sunlight from its stones, it presented a grandly awful prospect. Even Myddleton, who found the Middle Ages uncomfortable, could not help being struck by the solemnity of the site, and was impelled to further exploration.

He felt his way cautiously over the tumbled stones and irregular clumps towards the chancel. At least one of the tomb slabs was intact, raised a few inches from the floor and bearing an inscription, although the light did not enable him to decipher this. Surprisingly, in view of the ruinous state of the fabric and the long centuries of Scottish Calvinism, the altar itself seemed to be undamaged, and clear of the otherwise ubiquitous vegetation. There might even be some remnants of carving left, and Myddleton started poking about in the shrubbery.

He found, quickly enough, not fragments of delicate tracery or some desecrated portion of statuary but a dead cat. A black cat, not too long deceased – although he was no expert in these things – its fur bedraggled and jowls drawn back in an expiring rictus of agony. He hastily covered up the unpleasant object and cut short his visit to the ruined chapel, spending the rest of the evening writing up the notes he had previously made.

The next morning was spent in photographing and measuring the principal rooms. Gillespie had volunteered to hold the tape, since Myddleton was insistent on checking actual against recorded measurements. Careful mensuration had before now revealed inexpert alterations or additions to the original work, and an art historian who claimed to be authoritative could not neglect these.

At lunch-time they made their way to the village pub, which proved, as so often is the case on the Scottish side of the Border, a comfortless hostelry, with a surly and grubby landlord, which ran only to fizzy beer and chopped ham baps. These were however fresh, and must be made to serve.

Myddleton took the opportunity to ask Gillespie about the chapel: the schoolmaster had the information at his fingertips, and was pleased to display it. 'As you probably know, until the Reformation Peddie was a convent of the Praemonstratensians. It wasn't one of the best, and got itself a bad reputation in the later visitations. There were a lot of complaints about unnatural practices and sorcery, and the monks were unpopular with the locals, which was unusual, for in spite of what we Presbyterians like to think monasteries did their share of good works in their neighbourhoods, however badly they may have behaved within their own walls.

'The original buildings survived the Reformation, which is also unusual, for there wasn't an intact medieval building left anywhere else in Scotland, apart from the odd castle. This must have been something to do with the Peddies who bought the property. They had a reputation for holding their own, and woe betide those who challenged them. Apparently they liked to keep things as they were, and they preserved the conventional buildings. The chapel was used, too, until the end of the seventeenth century, but fell into ruins thereafter.'

'And this was the same family that built the present house?' asked Myddleton.

'Yes, and there's a funny thing here. Although the later Peddies kept every scrap of paper after 1765, when the New

Hall was built, I haven't been able to find anything referring to the medieval buildings.'

'And why is that?' Myddleton queried, 'Did they perhaps give them to a library?'

'None that I have been able to trace. It's my belief they were made away with, and I'll tell you the reason.'

Gillespie's glass was empty, and Myddleton did what was expected. The schoolmaster pulled his chair nearer and looked around. There were no other customers, but the landlord was about, looking studiously unconcerned.

'The witchcraft, or whatever it was, didn't die out with the monks. There was a seventeenth-century Peddie, who turned up at the beginning of the Bishops War. He'd been abroad, a soldier in the Thirty Years War, and was a great scoundrel. You'll see a reference to him in the Haddington annals, as a man renowned even among those violent men for cruelty and savagery. He was certainly present at the sack of Magdeburg, and you know what that means!'

Myddleton nodded; the Irish still complained about Drogheda and Wexford, but those were vicarage tea-parties compared with the horror of the sack of Magdeburg by the Catholic Imperialists, which had left the world aghast for generations.

'He wasn't the head of the family, or even a near relation, but suspiciously soon after he came back from the wars everyone standing between him and the property was dead or had disappeared. My information all comes from the public records: as I told you, there are no family papers at all. This William Peddie was deeply involved in sinister practices, but was never tried, although many people attempted to bring him to justice. There were all the usual things, black masses and the rest, and he was said to have access to a powerful familiar demon who would come from the corners of the universe to perpetrate whatever nastiness William wanted, and to protect him against the consequences.

'It must have been effective, his familiar, for Peddie lived to a considerable age, and until some time after Dutch William came over. Possibly because of his activities, the family found themselves quite rich and pulled down the old abbey, building the house you see now after the lapse of a couple of generations – which is about as long as a Scots family needs to make up its mind to try something new.'

'How very interesting,' said Myddleton, somewhat inaccurately, for he found that sort of Gothick horror too absurd to take seriously.

Gillespie looked at him closely, and made that sound peculiar to the Borders that may signify an infinite varity of guarded emotions, generally represented as 'mphmph'. 'Aye, you are probably right to be dubious. But what people believe to be a fact *is* a fact, you know, if it influences them strongly enough.'

Before they left, Gillespie absented himself for a few minutes. Seeing Myddleton alone, the landlord beckoned to him. 'Ga canny roon the auld hoose, mister. It's gey unchancy place. Ye wadna catch me theer at neet, all alone.' Myddleton was a little baffled, but caught the gist of the warning and made a polite acknowledgement.

The afternoon passed as busily as the morning, and it looked very much as though the work would be finished within the time originally specified, so that Myddleton would be able to go south again on the following day. Happily, only one more meal of Jennie's would need to be faced.

The light had stayed good and he had taken some photographs that he believed would be excellent: there was a Piranesi-like quality in the chiaroscuro. Gillespie's records, which were very full for the period after the building of the house, would write up well: it was only annoying that no reference to James Adam could be found. Presumably the building records had been destroyed with the earlier history.

Myddleton's intentions were altered just as he was settling down to the first whisky of the evening. Gillespie telephoned in some excitement. 'I didn't say anything earlier, for fear of raising false hopes, but I may have found a lead to Adam. When I heard you were coming I spoke to a friend of mine in the library of the Royal Incorporations – that's the Scottish Architects' Institute, you see. Well, they've never got their library properly organized – they found some original Robert Adam drawings in the attics only a year or two ago. My friend has just telephoned to say that there's a packet there that may include some of brother James's work – he'll have it out for you tomorrow if you'd like to have a look. It'll mean another day, but I'll drive you there and back. There are a few wee messages I should do, so it's no bother.'

This was indeed exciting. Not only did the prospect offer the hope of definitely identifying the designer of Peddie, but some new Adam drawings would be good for at least a couple of articles. Myddleton eagerly accepted Gillespie's offer and prepared to tackle Jennie's funeral baked meats with a better appetite.

He was, however, careful to make no further sorties in the direction of the chapel. The landlord, if he had properly understood him, was right: it was an unpleasant place. But an exploration of the domestic quarters might be in order, for during the day he and Gillespie had restricted themselves to the public rooms, the only areas likely to be of major interest. There were sometimes interesting items to be found elsewhere: he remembered an Irish house with a complete and magnificent early nineteenth-century laundry, abandoned shortly after its installation as being incomprehensible to the County Mayo staff. No such treats proved to be in store at Peddie: the domestic offices had been thoroughly modernized when the school had moved in, and no trace remained of the earlier fittings.

Since he had the house to himself, Myddleton thought he might as well walk around the girls' dormitories placed on the second floor. The action was not without a prurient element, for there is something about a number of girls, especially adolescent girls, living together, that any man, even one as sexually ambivalent as Myddleton, finds fascinating. Since this was the long vacation the girls had been gone for some weeks, and none of their personal belongings were to be seen, but the atmosphere of the rooms, the mysterious, secretive femaleness of it all, was redolent almost of a different species. He could imagine small naked feet scurrying, whispers and laughter.

It was not until he regained the secure anonymity of the visitors' room that he recalled the bare altar and the dead cat. Could some occult practices still be carried on there? He had read of such things, and remembered that they were often connected with puberty ceremonies and adolescence. It was an unwelcome thought, and he banished it with a large whisky.

When Edinburgh was reached the following day the drawings turned out to be of real interest. They were unmistakably Adam, as the pen-work over an invisible framework of scored and pencilled lines, the graduated ink washes, and the careful lettering proved. The house was also almost certainly Peddie, although the elevations seemed to have been altered. The Incorporation generously provided him with photostats, and Myddleton left, a contented art historian.

Gillespie was taking some time over his 'messages' and as Myddleton had an hour or two to spare he determined to spend it in that small but excellent collection, the National Gallery of Scotland, on the Mound.

He had been there many times before and strolled around, ignoring most of the paintings and spending time with his favourites and with the new acquisitions. He was just moving to that extraordinary El Greco of the two boys and the monkey, when his attention was drawn by a small Dutch painting. At first glance this seemed nothing more than the conventional church interior that one sees in so many seventeenth-century paintings, but a moment's inspection proved it otherwise. The painting was by Van Steenwyck and showed the east end of a church with a rite in progress round the altar; no Christian service, but the adoration of a huge crowned figure brightly illuminated by candles. On the lefthand side, in what would be the north transept, men and women were celebrating some sort of lascivious orgy, and on the right, advancing towards the viewer were two figures. One was a man carrying a torch followed by another menacing form, the lineaments of which were indistinct in the torchlight but which threatened to be of a horrible monstrosity.

And the most surprising thing, that made Myles perceptibly start, was that the church was identical with the chapel at Peddie. There could be no doubt of it: it was complete rather than ruinous, but most certainly an accurate representation of the chapel. To the trained eye the quadripartite rib-vaults and the distinctive arrangement of the liernes were conclusive.

What was more, the impression that this was a picture done from life was overwhelming: no imaginary composition but a precise depiction of a closely observed scene, or series of scenes. The painter had seen what he had painted – Myddleton was convinced of it: the terrible figure preceded by the torch-bearer had advanced towards him as it advanced now, moving out of the painting.

It was extremely unpleasant: Myddleton left the Gallery in some haste and was glad to be out in the chill Edinburgh sun.

He was quiet on the return journey, which was a disappointment to Gillespie who had expected his discovery to provoke a more enthusiastic reception and who consequently left Myddleton at the Hall with a cool farewell.

Myddleton was containing his excitement with difficulty. If the Peddie chapel was indeed depicted in the Van Steenwyck it would constitute an artistic discovery of some magnitude: the picture might even become known as the Myddleton Steenwyck. Bouncing out of the car, and paying scant attention to Gillespie's distant good-bye, he made first for his bedroom, then for the housekeeper's room, where he armed himself with a wire brush.

He had retrieved a Claude glass from his bedroom, a useful object which he took with him on all his travels. Arrived at the ruins, he stationed himself in a spot which he judged to be that from which the artist had painted the chapel, and adjusted the mirrors. Framed and softened in the glass, the image was unmistakable: it was indeed the Van Steenwyck chapel.

His next move was to the grave slab he had noticed on his previous visit. An archaeologist or a medievalist might have hesitated but an eighteenth-century rationalist loves a little clearing up, so Myddleton immediately busied himself with brushing away the lichen from the flat top of the tomb. A few minutes sufficed to reveal the inscription: it consisted, simply enough, of the initials GPVS, in large capitals, and the date MDCXCII.

All this was very satisfactory. In one day he had identified Peddie as an Adam house, discovered a hitherto unrecognized painting of its old chapel, and established a possible link between the picture and the weird goings-on of the wicked William Peddie. Was it not possible – the dates seemed to be compatible – that the picture represented an actual rite taking place on this very spot, and that the figure portrayed was Peddie himself, followed by his giant familiar? Moreover, although the significance of the initials was unclear to him, the date might well be that of William's death, and the tomb his.

Myddleton sat on the grave slab and pondered. If proof of the connection was to be found, the obvious place to look next was the tomb itself. Since this had originally been inside the church the slab probably covered a vault, decently lined with stone and provided with steps. An exploration would not, therefore, be excessively difficult. On the other hand it was a sinister place, and the idea of descending into a tomb, even a commodious and dry one, was not the cheeriest of prospects. Would not the assistance of Gillespie, even at the cost of sharing the discovery with him, be advisable?

The sight of the bare altar and the memory of the dead cat decided him. He recalled, too, that strange atmosphere in the girls' rooms and wondered at the connection. If traditions of witchcraft had either survived or been revived, some moral support was needed. He moved off with every appearance of decisiveness to telephone Gillespie.

As luck – bad luck for Myddleton – would have it the schoolmaster was not in. Myddleton left a message with Mrs Gillespie, asking her husband to drop in as soon as he returned as something interesting had cropped up.

It will be appreciated that Myles Myddleton was not a man given to decisive action: he sat down, looking at the telephone, and dithered. Not by any means brave or adventurous, Myles was nevertheless insatiably curious, a trait which had stood him in good stead as an art historian. At least, he thought, he might root out some tools which would be needed for the job.

A good torch was essential, and this he remembered seeing in the basement next to the bank of switches and fuse-boxes by the stillroom. He ran downstairs, glad that Jennie (and even more so, Mrs Margulies) would not be about to question him. Vaults are usually not too difficult to open, but a crowbar or jemmy would be needed. After a good deal of rummaging he found in an outhouse some metal stakes of the sort used for electric fencing, with one end sharply pointed.

When, later, Gillespie had still not turned up, Myddleton, anxious to finish the job before dark, moved off to the old chapel. Although the evening was still light enough, the ruins were in shadow and decidedly chill. A little hard work would assist with that.

As Myddleton had expected, the slab moved quite easily: if he had paused for reflection he might have considered it suspiciously easy, but the itch of unsatisfied curiosity was strong in him. Shining his light through the gap he had opened, Myles could see that there was indeed a flight of steps leading into what seemed to be a sizeable chamber.

Casting caution to the winds, he inserted himself into the hole and gingerly descended the stairs, watching carefully where he put his feet. Though amply wide and indefinitely long, the vault was not deep, and Myles, not a tall man, had to keep his head down. As a result he saw only what the torch disclosed lying immediately before him.

The first object, not unnaturally, was a coffin: a substantial affair of stone, bound with iron, and large enough to contain a lead lining. An inscription was discernable: GPVS again, and underneath CAVE CUSTODEM.

If Myddleton had been a better Latinist, or a quicker thinker, he would have been out of that vault sharper than he had come in, but as it was the meaning of the inscription escaped him, and he shone his torch around the chamber. The floor of the vault was a jumble of earth and stones: some of the latter were lighter in colour, and might well have been bones, so Myles did not dwell on them, but directed the beam towards the head of the coffin. And found the guardian.

A massive form, humanoid, covered in coarse black hair, sat crouched there. It was so large that the low roof confined the thing to a squatting position, its huge taloned hands resting on its knees, the gaunt features of its great head indistinguishable but horribly threatening. As Myles stood aghast, the creature emitted a hoarse rattle and moved its black hands towards him.

Gillespie proved himself a man of parts: he heard the scream as he was walking from his car, and rushed to the scene, guided by the torch which had fallen and was shining like a beacon out of the tomb.

It was some days before Myles, who made a good recovery, was ready to speak about his experience. Sitting in an easy chair in the schoolmaster's house, stayed with hot milk and comforted with whisky, he began diffidently, 'Stupid of me really, to go poking about like that.'

Gillespie agreed. 'Aye, I'd not counsel grave-breaking as a healthy occupation, especially when alone, and you being of a nervous disposition.'

'I can't even remember what I did find,' (the truth was that

182

Myddleton had no wish to call to mind that appalling vision).
'Did you see the inscription?'

'I did, and you'd have maybe been better off if you'd done the same.'

'What was it, then?'

In his best pedantic fashion Gillespie proceeded. 'The initials were obvious enough. G – Guilliemus or William, P – Peddie, S – *Sepultus est.*'

'Oh, yes,' murmured the abashed Myles, 'Of course.'

'I can understand that the V might cause a moment's hesitation: it's a not too common word – *veneficus*, a sorcerer. *Magus* is more common, as you know, but *veneficus* has a stronger connotation of evil. It was, however, the subscription, which could hardly be simpler, that might have given one pause. Do you not recall "*Cave custodem*: beware of the guardian"?'

Myles sank back in his chair: oh yes, he did remember, only too clearly. 'Was there – look – I'm sure I saw something really awful down there – was there anything that – shouldn't have been?'

Gillespie poured them both a little more whisky. 'It's very easy to imagine things in such conditions, but in fact there were some extraordinarily large bones there. Shall I tell you what I believe to be the truth of the matter?'

Myddleton did not trust himself to speak, but nodded assent.

'You may remember that the wicked William had spent his youth in the German wars, and was said to have a monstrous familiar. Let us connect those two facts, and posit that William procured the services of a real giant – not uncommon in Central Europe, as Frederick of Prussia proved only a little later. William would have kept his giant hidden away, the better to terrify his neighbours, and would only have allowed him to appear in such ambiguous circumstances as would enable the superstitious peasants of this region to believe in a demon summoned by the wizard Peddie.

'When the giant died – such creatures do not live long – Peddie buried him, and perhaps kept up the pretence of a familiar demon with a few conjuring tricks. When his own turn came, William had himself interred in the same vault. I looked at the bones there, and they were certainly human, but very large. He must have been nearly eight feet tall. And there was a lot of hair, which is not unnatural either. The skeleton was held together by a linen binding, and, given the fact that he'd been squashed into a confined space, it was quite possible that when you shone your light you saw the remains of what – dead or alive – must have been a frightful monstrosity.'

Myddleton was extremely relieved, but a doubt remained. 'Silly of me, I know, but I could have sworn the thing moved towards me – oh, very nasty, it was. And, well, spoke.'

Gillespie surveyed him gravely. 'Rats.'

Myles was offended. 'No, really, I'm sure that damned thing moved. And I heard a noise. Quite distinctly.'

'Oh, likely enough.' Gillespie permitted himself a smile. 'But rats, all the same. There were a number of them about, and indeed there always have been some savage beasts round Peddie. Even some of the cats have been killed. They'd probably made themselves at home in the skeleton, were startled when you shone the light at them, and jumped out of the way. They're heavy beasts, and might have made it lurch forward rather nastily.'

Myles considered the matter and decided that he would regard this as an acceptable explanation: there was, after all, still an excellent article to be worked up, and neither *Country Life* nor the *Connoisseur* could be expected warmly to welcome necrophiles or necromants. His decision was eminently sensible, and should serve as an example to those who might otherwise be tempted to enquire too deeply into matters best left quite alone.